OUT of THE
DEVIL'S
MOUTH

TRAVIS THRASHER

OUT of THE DEVIL'S MOUTH

A Henry Wolfe Adventure

MOODY PUBLISHERS
CHICAGO

Editor: LB Norton
Interior Design: LeftCoast Design
Cover Design: Kirk Douponce, Dog Eared Design
Cover Image (canoe): Superstock

Library of Congress Cataloging-in-Publication Data

Thrasher, Travis, 1971-
  Out of the devil's mouth / Travis Thrasher.
    p. cm. — (A Henry Wolfe adventure)
  ISBN-13: 978-0-8024-8669-1
  ISBN-10: 0-8024-8669-X
  1. Missionaries—Fiction. I. Title.

  PS3570.H6925O98 2008
  813'.54—dc22

                                        2007049244

We hope you enjoy this book from Moody Publishers. Our goal is to provide high-qual-
ity, thought-provoking books and products that connect truth to your real needs and
challenges. For more information on other books and products written and produced
from a biblical perspective, go to www.moodypublishers.com or write to:

Moody Publishers
820 N. LaSalle Boulevard
Chicago, IL 60610

1 3 5 7 9 10 8 6 4 2

Printed in the United States of America

To Andy McGuire,
for stories told and untold

CHICAGO

Winter of 1928

It was November, just a few days before Thanksgiving, the ground hard and the city sidewalks sprinkled with a light snow, and I truly didn't know if I was going to live to see turkey and dressing. I had just finished up a night with the boys down at a joint on the north side when four men grabbed me and shoved me into a car. The gun against my gut helped. Fifteen minutes later I found myself outside under a glowing moon, watching my breath as I marched over train tracks near the large rail yard.

I knew what it was about, of course.

"Can I just have a chance to talk with Moran?" I asked.

The men didn't want to talk. The only words they had said were "Shut up" and "Keep walking."

"This is something that can be cleared up over a few drinks, fellas. Let's just think about this."

We were on the outskirts of the city near the Chicago River. They were working on straightening out the river, something I had been reading about in the papers, so the entire area was littered with machinery and frozen mud and vehicles and train tracks. Bright, cold light from the moon illuminated the silent railroad cars around us.

"Any reason we're here?" I asked.

"Any reason you can't shut your mouth?" the biggest of the bunch shot back.

They all looked alike in their long coats and fedoras. I wondered about the fashion sense of a whole nation of hat donning, coat wearing men with their hair slicked back. I myself didn't have a hat tonight and needed a haircut and wore a short wool coat.

We crossed a road, deserted and barren. The men acted like they knew exactly where we were headed.

"Don't slow down," ordered a deep voice, apparently that of the man shoving the gun at my back.

"The article wasn't that bad," I said. "It mentioned Bugs. So what? There are a dozen articles a day pointing fingers at Capone. What's wrong with one little story?"

"Take a right," the gunman said.

"We getting on a train?"

"One of us is," the smallest of the group taunted.

A couple of them laughed at his comment.

"The city looks nice from down here, doesn't it?" I said.

The guy with the gun stepped up next to me as we walked. "Do you realize you're about to die, mister?"

"It's Henry. And yes, I'm getting that idea."

"Then don't make this any worse than it needs to be."

I laughed. "Tell me something, 'mister.' Is there anything worse than death?"

He waved his gun for me to keep the pace.

"I'm just wondering if it's going to be by land or by sea?"

"That's cute," he said. "Keep it up."

"Look—you stuff me in one of those boxcars, some wandering vagabond will come upon me and lose whatever little lunch he had. Then he'll report it. That's no good for you guys."

"Head toward the bridge."

I could hear the shuffling of our feet as we walked toward the truss bridge that allowed trains to pass over the Chicago River. I could see the crisscross of the dark beams against the glow of the moonlight.

"Not the river—it's way too cold, boys. Give a man a break."

"You might be dead before you hit the water," the shorter, weasel-faced guy said.

"Well, that's comforting."

"Keep walking."

"Guys, look. You're family men, right?"

"Nope." It was the deep-voiced gunman.

"Uh-uh," the big guy added.

The weasel-like man only laughed, his head bobbing slightly.

"Hardly" was the fourth man's comment.

I cleared my throat. "Yeah, well, me neither. Women, who needs them, huh?"

"Are you going to grovel, Henry?" deep voice asked.

"No. I don't grovel. What's your name?"

"It doesn't matter."

"I'd like to know the name of the man who is going to kill me."

"You already do," he said quickly. "You wrote a nice tell-all article about his business dealings in Chicago."

"Yes. Because I write. I'm a *writer*, not a killer. Not a threat. Just a writer."

"You're supposed to be an adventurer, right?" said the weasel. "You wrote that book about Egypt?"

"Yes, of course. I can get you an autographed copy if we go back to my place."

"A bunch of lies, if you ask me. How did you get out of that pyramid alone, huh?"

"So you're a critic, huh?" I asked, looking at his narrow face. "Look, you don't have to shoot me because you didn't like my book."

"My girlfriend told me to read it. She said, 'Jack, you need to read this because it's unbelievable.'"

"Stop talking," said the guy with the gun.

"Look, Jack—everything I wrote in that book was true."

"Who told you my name?" he asked.

"Shut up! Both of you! Start heading over the bridge. Now!"

I could hear the water below me. The tracks I stepped over felt ragged and hard.

If this was going to be my night to die, it would be a beautiful one. Not too windy, the chill so achingly silent and still. There were worse places to meet one's end.

"Gentlemen, there has to be a better solution than this," I said.

I knew it was close to midnight, and the good times I had

enjoyed with the boys tonight were long gone. I heard the footsteps following me.

"Anybody have a cigarette?" I asked.

"You're not getting one."

So much for that idea.

If I could grab one of the men and try for his gun—no way.

I kept walking, the moon reflecting off the dark water below me.

"I really don't have anything against Bugs," I said.

"Unfortunately, he wants you dead, Mr. Wolfe," the gunman said.

"Mr. Wolfe sounds so formal."

"Nothing formal about this."

We had reached the middle of the bridge.

"Stop there," the gunman told me.

I could feel sweat against my neck and back.

I breathed in.

This was going to hurt.

There were four of them. Wondering why it should take four men to kill an unarmed writer? I was wondering the same thing. I figured one would actually do the killing, while another would watch his back, while a third man provided counseling afterwards (cigarette, meaningless guy talk, a nod of a job well done, and a realization that he could have never done it himself), and the fourth would—well, I wasn't sure what the fourth would do. Drive the getaway car? What exactly would they be getting away from?

"Stop here," the big guy said.

"Didn't you just say that?" I asked. "I'm not going anywhere."

"Just do what we say," the gunman said, waving the weapon as if to remind me it was still there.

So far I hadn't even looked at his gun. Not straight on, that is. Maybe if I ignored it long enough, it would go away.

I turned around but kept toward the center of the bridge, standing between the rails. I slowed down but didn't actually stop.

"I said stop."

"Guys—look. I'm not much of a swimmer," I lied.

One of them laughed. I turned to see it was the weasel, his smile almost touching his ears.

"Who says you're going to be swimming?"

"I'd call it more like bobbing," said number four guy.

Ah, now I knew why he was there. The fourth man provided comic relief.

"If I could just get a chance to meet with Moran," I said.

"Isn't going to happen," the big guy said.

"I can slip out of Chicago unnoticed."

"That's our job," funny guy said.

The big guy kept talking. "He wants to make a statement. And you're the statement."

I stood facing the men, one holding a gun at my chest, another smiling at me, another smoking a cigarette, and the fourth looking into the distance.

"Look—okay. Just—if you could take Bugs a message. From me."

"Yeah, what would that be?"

I stared at all the men and then focused on the big guy. "Tell

Bugs I meant every word I wrote, and that I have a lot more dirt to fling to the world if I want to."

I launched myself at the gunman and took him by surprise. My body rammed his arm and sent it pointing sideways, getting off a shot that tore through the night. Both of us lost our footing and slammed to the ground, the gunman cushioning my fall as he let out a moan. The other three men scrambled, but I didn't wait to see their reactions. I let go of the hulking figure I'd smashed into and kept running toward an opening in the steel beams of the bridge. I catapulted off and hoped the water below was deep enough for a head-first dive.

I also hoped there wasn't anything in the water. Like a broken piece of machinery or an old rusted-out engine or anything that would really, really hurt to crash into. With my head.

Even though I was in the air for less than a second, I could hear a voice calling out behind me. The splash of the cold water drowned out the noise. For several moments everything went black. The cold stopped my heart, my breathing, my thoughts.

There was nothing in the water except lifeless chill.

My eyes tightened shut as I went deep, deeper into the river water.

I instantly started swimming to my left, staying at the level I was at. I felt something rubbing up against me. Something gentle, like plants or light debris. I wasn't afraid of a strange creature below in the frigid darkness. I was afraid of a wandering bullet piercing my skull.

I flung my feet and pumped my hands. I'm a good swimmer and can hold my breath for a long time. I didn't know the width of the river or how deep I was, but I kept swimming to try to find the shore.

Soon my lungs felt like they were about to burst. I managed to surface slowly and bob my head out of the water. My eyes opened, my entire body numb.

I thought of the large dinner I'd eaten, and wondered if my fate would be cramping up and drowning because of a pork chop.

Voices shouted above me. I saw the figures rushing to each side of the bridge, two men coming toward my side of the river.

"Hey! Right there!"

A set of gunshots erupted in the still night. I dived back under water, having gotten my bearings. I was about fifty yards from the shore. I swam as hard as I ever had in my life toward the land.

Soon I felt ground below my hands and knees. I got on my feet and ran out of the river onto a muddy bank. I heard a few more shots, but I couldn't tell if they were even close. I slipped and fell on my back into the slimy mud, quickly regained my footing, and sprinted toward the edge of the river and whatever lay beyond it.

Imagine a man in a suit and overcoat, drenched and muddy and breathless and scared white as a ghost. How fast can a man like that run? Pretty fast, if you ask me. And especially after taking the overcoat off and discarding it on the bank.

I'd always liked that coat. But I liked my life a little better.

The night air made it hard to breathe.

A pistol cracked in the night, and voices called out. What, did they think I was going to stop?

I reached the top of the bank and found a dirt road. I bolted off toward the shadowy forms of the sleeping railroad cars. I had no idea where in the world I was going, but I needed to get somewhere else fast.

In the boxcar, darkness enveloped me. I quietly shivered as I sat, my arms tight around my bent legs, my face buried in my damp arms. I couldn't stop shaking. My soaked clothes were stiff and heavy. I tried to calm down my breathing, and my nerves, and remain as silent as possible. I knew the men were still outside, looking for me, waiting to hear the slightest bit of noise, ready to use their guns.

I recalled a time when I was colder than this. It was during that ill-advised Antarctic expedition, the one that never really got going. Now that was cold. A death cold, the sort that made you stay awake for fear of meeting your Maker with the slightest brush of the eyelids.

Memories like that are good; they put things into perspective. Yes, I was cold, but this was nothing like that sort of cold. And yes, I was in danger of my life, but all I needed to do was remain hidden and I'd be fine.

Slow-moving footsteps could be heard coming closer to the boxcar. They stopped directly outside the large, empty car. There was nothing inside except darkness. And me, shivering and crouching like a wounded animal as its hunters approached.

I watched the head in the opening, his fedora outlined in the faint night light. He stood for a moment, looking in the car, seemingly right at me, then he continued on.

The question now was how long to wait.

Some voices called out, and an answering voice startled me with its closeness.

"Yeah, yeah, hold on!"

The figure reappeared at the entrance of the car.

He climbed up the ladder and stood in the entryway.

"Come on, I know you're in here," he said.

I released my arms from my legs and shifted my weight back. I slowly rose. I was in the corner to the man's right. I knew he couldn't see me, but he might hear me.

I didn't breathe as I rose.

"Interesting how the edge of this car is wet. Not too smart, are you, Henry?"

I stepped toward him, my body hunched over, ready to attack. I waited until I saw his face looking the other way, the outline of his body revealing the pointed barrel of a gun.

With only a few yards to reach him, I rushed over and swung my fist toward his head. Luckily, it struck the bone of his cheek.

When you're not expecting a full-throttled hit against the jaw, believe me, it hurts.

He let out a deep howl as he dropped his gun and was sent back against the wall of the train car. I reached for him and grabbed his neck with one arm, my other hand finding his mouth.

He doubled over as I held his mouth.

"Don't say a word," I whispered.

He was the smallest of the men, the weasel with the big mouth, so thankfully I could keep him in one place.

I released his mouth and felt the ground around us. I came across the automatic pistol and picked it up, forcing the gun into his mouth. The barrel fit there perfectly.

"This wouldn't taste good if I pressed the trigger," I said. "So keep quiet."

In a few moments the other men started calling out his name.

"Don't be stupid, Jack," I said.

He nodded and breathed heavily and swallowed as I kept the gun in his mouth.

Another figure approached the boxcar door and remained there for a second.

The man tensed, but I stuck the gun down further. I started to shake again and couldn't stop it.

"Jack, come on! Where are you? Jack?"

I realized I wasn't the only one shaking.

I took the gun out of his mouth once I could hear the men calling him in the distance.

"Stay in here for a minute. I'll use this on you. I promise."

Before I could hear him respond, I knocked him over the head with the butt of the pistol.

By the sound of the crumpling mass on the floor, I figured he wasn't going to go anywhere. Not for a while.

Now I needed to find a way out.

They spotted me running across the clearing of the railroad yard toward the hulking dark shadow of a moving train.

One bullet nearly found its way to my ankle. The few remaining shots were desperate last chances to make amends for their botched killing.

I sprinted next to the train, making sure I didn't trip as I grabbed on to the metal bars of a side ladder, and then held firm as the train picked up speed.

As the men rushed toward me in the distance, their dark figures merely thumbprints against the murky light of the train yard, I waved at them.

I wasn't sure where this train was going, but I knew one thing.

I needed to get out of Chicago, and fast.

As I clung to the ladder and felt the night air chill me, the wheels below making a methodical clanking, I finally breathed out a sigh of relief.

Little did I know I had begun my journey to the Devil's Mouth.

NEW YORK CITY

The door was like any door on any street in the city. Unlit, nondescript, seemingly deserted. The figure stepped out of the shadowy doorway and filled it with his immense physique, as if to block my way.

"I'm here to see Arthur Holden," I said.

The man didn't move for a minute. Eyes I couldn't see stared me down. Then he moved and allowed me access without saying a word. I slipped through a set of heavy, dark curtains and entered the speakeasy.

It was loud and smoky, and I studied the faces as I walked past tables. I found him waiting in a small booth, glassy eyes showing he had been here awhile. He shook my hand as I slipped into the booth and faced him.

"You're a hard man to track down," I said.

"And I hear you're a hard man to kill."

"I have a knack for getting out of tough places. I've learned from the best."

"Your nine lives will catch up with you sooner or later, Henry."

"Are you calling me a cat? I hate cats."

"I do too, but I can't seem to get rid of the ones my wife keeps bringing home."

I laughed as a waitress brought me a drink. It was heavier and not as smooth as I was used to, but that was fine. I wasn't here for the drinks. I was here for the man across from me, whose face was lit by an orange glow.

"I hear you could use some work," Arthur said eventually.

"I hear you're desperate for some good writers."

"Always! The world is full of many things, Henry, but talented writers are not one of them."

Arthur Holden would know. He'd spent a decade working in the newspaper business, even once working in the same office as I did in Chicago. He was my boss, and one of my claims to fame is to have survived him. Arthur's gift was cutting. Extraneous verbiage, unnecessary adjectives, useless employees—Arthur didn't care what he cut. If it needed to go, it went. He was a terrible manager, a horrible husband, atrocious at managing his money, but he could take an article and rework it for the common man in an utterly brilliant way. He said he had always like my style—easy to read, no nonsense, unpretentious. He really, really hated pretension.

"You don't want to work with writers," I once told him. "You want to work with words. Forget the idiots who pen them."

He laughed and agreed.

The last time I had seen him was over a year ago when he enlisted me to write an article about Chicago murders for *Time* magazine, where he worked now.

"Your last assignment nearly got me killed," I told him.

"They were just trying to scare you."

I sipped my drink and shook my head. I opened my mouth to say something, then just waited, glaring at him.

Arthur was sweaty—the man was always, always sweaty. He had an ample forehead with thinning hair slicked back, a neck way too thick for its shirt. He had an intensity about him that put the fear of God into young writers. The list was long of fledgling newcomers cut down by Arthur's pen and posture. They usually never got the chance to see his grin. Once you saw that smile, you knew he couldn't be all bad. And it was that smile that beamed on his face now.

"So tell me something," he said. "How would you like to go on an adventure?"

I laughed. "Anywhere but Chicago."

*A*rthur ordered another drink and took his time enjoying it. For me, drinking has always been a formality, part of the game you play with men and society. But for Arthur, it was something else entirely. For him, it was as necessary as the act of breathing. For a moment, as he sipped from a glass that had just replaced another empty one, he seemed lost in his own world. Then he came back to reality.

"First New York, then Chicago," he said.

"New York was different, and you know it."

"What? No women involved back in Chi-town?"

"Not this time. Someone less dangerous. Just the mob."

Arthur liked my joke.

"So you up for another expedition?"

Up for another expedition? That's exactly what the telegram from Arthur had asked, the one I'd received just the day before I was almost killed by Moran's goons.

"Depends on where it might be."

"How about south?"

"South of what?"

"America."

"I'm intrigued. Haven't been down there in a few years."

"You're going to want to go on this trip. Could be your next bestseller."

"Arthur, has anybody ever told you that you look like a schoolboy when you've got something up your sleeve?"

He laughed. "Then I must look like a schoolboy all the time."

"I'd agree. Just a little heavier, sweatier, with a bad drinking problem."

This made him laugh harder. He composed himself, looked around the loud joint to see if anyone was watching, then moved his head toward me as if he was about to tell me some deep, dark secret.

"How much do you know about Colonel Fawcett?"

"I know enough," I replied. "He and a couple of men, one of them his son, went exploring in the jungles in Brazil and were never heard from again."

"Boy, as a storyteller, you get an F."

"You like straight to the point, right?"

His ruddy skin glowed in the dim light. Arthur nodded, then decided to add to my unsatisfactory story.

"Fawcett believed there was an ancient city hidden away in the middle of the Matto Grosso. They say there is hidden gold in the heart of the jungle, that there are white Indians who speak English and mystic powers that go beyond anything anyone has seen."

"I've read a lot about the Colonel."

"Then you'll know that Fawcett and his men disappeared on their quest back in '25."

"There are reports that he's still alive."

Arthur nodded. "And there have been expeditions that have gone off in search of him."

I had an idea where all of this was going. "So, what? Is there another expedition setting off? To search for Fawcett?"

"Not exactly."

I waited while he finished his drink and rubbed his eyes.

"Most people believed Fawcett and his men died in the wilderness. I'm one of them. Probably killed by Indians or from the conditions. A handful of explorers have said they've run across a man they believe to be Fawcett, but those claims have usually been proven wrong. Usually just someone wanting to tell a tall tale for a buck."

"Sounds like someone I know," I said.

"You ever hear of the Prescott family?"

"Arthur, I haven't been living in South America. Everybody has heard of the Prescott family. Especially anyone living in New York or Chicago."

"Then you know they're rich. Stanley Prescott has enough money to buy and do anything he wants. Banking and real estate have really paid off. Know much about the family?"

"They live in New York, right? Several children. He's in the news a lot. That's about it."

"Five children, to be exact. Four boys and a girl. All adults, of course. The second eldest is Louis, almost thirty years old. Close to your age, huh?"

"I'm twenty-seven."

"About time you became an adult. Happy birthday and all that. About a year ago, Louis Prescott set off on an expedition to find Fawcett. Quite an expedition, too."

"Really? I never heard anything about it."

"It was very discreet. The Prescotts are a private family for the most part. They don't like people knowing about their affairs unless it's good for business. My understanding is that for Louis, this was an adventure, the kind he always wanted to take, the kind he read about in books like yours. He's like you—except without all the debt or someone trying to kill him. They mounted quite the operation to find Fawcett, or find out what happened to him. And to uncover the legendary lost city in the jungle."

"And what's this have to do with you?" I asked.

He nodded. "We helped organize the expedition."

I sat up and leaned over the table. "We?"

"The magazine thought it would be a good story to cover."

"Okay. So a rich kid took an expedition to South America. What's the story in that? And why the secrecy?"

Arthur's face settled into a contemplative shadow, a mask hiding something dark.

"What do you know about the fountain of youth?"

My grandfather used to take me to a creek down the winding road near our home. Deep in the heart of Tennessee, where I spent most of my childhood. We'd bring a pail of rocks, and he'd tell me to make a wish before I threw each one. After he got sick, I'd go down there by myself and throw rocks into the slow, trickling water. Every single wish was that Papa would get better. But the wishes didn't get answered.

"The fountain of youth, huh?" I asked. "It's one of those classic myths. Some claim they found it in Florida."

"The expedition that Louis Prescott led to find Fawcett took a new direction when that trail grew cold and Louis discovered something else. He heard detailed reports of a tribe of Indians with a massive dwelling, perhaps underground, deep in the mountains of the Matto Grosso. He heard that some missionaries had stumbled across this city. And every report said that this group of Indians had conquered death and found eternal life."

"And Louis believed this? Did you guys believe this?"

"The expedition was already well underway, and it took a whole new direction. But it's difficult getting any sort of contact once you're that removed from civilization. We got a few telegrams, a couple notes. Some of the reports made wild claims. Everything Louis discovered led him to something else. He believed that Fawcett might have stumbled upon the same thing, and that the explorer might be alive."

"I'm guessing the fountain of youth wasn't discovered," I said.

"Louis disappeared." Arthur took a drink. "For nine months there hasn't been a word. The Prescott family led an expedition that ended up disbanding after trails led to nothing. Louis and his men disappeared, just like Fawcett."

"So are you wanting *me* to disappear, Arthur?"

He laughed. "This is a big story, my boy. One that needs to be documented. So far it hasn't leaked out, Louis Prescott disappearing. But it's going to. And when it does—well, it'd be nice to have the main story, wouldn't it?"

"Yes, it would. It would also be nice to stay alive to write more stories."

"Listen. The Prescott family is mounting another expedition, this time trying for publicity. And they want you to cover it."

"May I ask why me?"

"Because I told them you're one of the best in the business."

"One of how many?"

"And because Stanley Prescott happens to be a big fan of your Egypt book."

"Good thing he didn't ask me to go with Louis and his group."

"There's another angle to the story."

I leaned back in my seat. "Of course there is."

"We spent some time digging around, asking locals and Indians about this lost city. The notion of a lost city in the Amazon jungle isn't anything new, but the story of a tribe that's conquered death—now *that* is a tale. And it kept coming up again and again."

"The only way I know of conquering death is to tell a tale. One that's good enough to last centuries."

"This could be it for you, Henry. They kept hearing a phrase the natives used to describe a place—a city, a village, whatever. A place not on the map. They called it the Devil's Mouth."

"The Devil's Mouth?" I repeated. "What's that mean?"

Arthur shook his head. "I believe that there is a city or a place—a civilization—that is out there, and this Devil's Mouth is the key to finding it. I want you to find it, Henry. Or find if it's just another tall tale. You found that lost pyramid, didn't you? Who would ever have thought something like that could happen? You can find a lost city in the jungle."

"And then write about it for you?"

"Lead story in *Time*. You get as much coverage as necessary. Could be in installments. With another book deal for you."

"What's my fee for going on this suicide mission?"

"The Prescott family said name your price."

I nodded. Considering my sorry state of financial affairs and the fact that I needed to lie low for a while, this sounded like an answer to prayer.

But I wasn't a praying man. And it sounded also like playing Russian roulette with more than one bullet.

"You know, Arthur, when I heard from you, I thought you were just contacting an old friend."

"I told Stanley Prescott two things about you, Henry. First, you have this knack of finding things that have been buried or hidden away."

"And second?"

"To keep his daughter far away from you."

"South America should be far enough, don't you think?"

Something in Arthur's face twinkled, as though he were holding a royal flush in his hands and the pot was big. "Maybe not."

For a few moments we talked about financials, a topic I always hated but which paid for those wonderful things like food and rent. Actually, I would have gone for free, and Arthur knew it. Talking about money was just a formality. I couldn't go back to Chicago, not now, not for a while.

There was something in the way Arthur talked that said he wasn't telling me everything.

"You're keeping something from me, Arthur."

"Yes. I'm just—I'm trying to figure out how to say this."

"Just get it out."

"We need you to get Max for this trip."

I let out a laugh. "Even I can't do that."

"The Prescotts want him. They've asked for both of you. He knows the country, Henry. He'd be useful, for a lot of reasons."

"Oh, sure. Useful getting us killed. He's not in prime shape, last I heard. I think he's in about the same shape as you. Why don't you just come instead?"

"Max is in a different league. The two of you demonstrated your abilities in Egypt."

I shook my head. "You know, sometimes I think there's a curse to having a bestseller everybody's read."

"It's your claim to fame, Henry."

"Well, Max has squandered most of his fame. And claims."

"He's in Key West. You need to find him."

"Uh-uh. It's not going to happen. I haven't spoken to Max in a couple of years. He won't be happy to see me."

"He was your professor, your mentor."

"Yeah, well—we didn't leave things too well. You know what happened."

"This could be the biggest story of your life."

I shook my head and breathed in. "It'll be easier finding the fountain of youth than recruiting Max to come along with me for another adventure."

In my hotel room, I examined the faded and creased photograph. I carried it around everywhere, more as a good luck piece than anything else.

In the photo were Max, tall and lean with short gray hair and a wry smile, and me, laughing at something he had said.

In between us stood Kalila, the Egyptian beauty Max had fallen for, and fallen hard.

Yes, that Kalila.

She smiled like a shy schoolgirl, yet her dark eyes and glowing skin revealed a remarkably complex and unquestionably striking young woman.

Staring at the photo, I wondered what Max would say when he saw me again. And whether he still blamed me for Kalila's death.

KEY WEST

Max Joubert?"

The taxi driver only shook his head.

"Max Joubert?"

The innkeeper looked at me as though he didn't know that was a name.

"Max Joubert?"

The bartender didn't answer. And he didn't even bother to look at the black-and-white photograph I placed on the bar in front of him. It showed a lean man in his fifties with a narrow face and warm, almond-shaped eyes. He had a controlled smile on his face. The Frenchman always carried secrets with him.

The biggest secret now was where Max actually was.

I came to the southernmost tip of the United States with simply a name and a photo. I didn't have an address, but I figured I didn't need one. People like Max don't go unnoticed for long. Their charms and their troubles often lead to their making a name for themselves very quickly. But so far, nobody wanted to share.

It was a warm afternoon, and I stayed in the bar for a drink. The beer tasted good. I stared at the picture of Max and wondered what my old teacher and mentor would do when he saw me again.

It would be impossible to take the trip without him. I had been in South America a few times, but never in the jungle. Max was a naturalist and had explored the Amazon jungle several times over, writing articles on various topics including an Indian tribe, the discovery of a new type of blue-fronted Amazon parrot, and surviving on your own. Max was the expert traveler; I had always been the happy sidekick, going along for the ride and later getting credit for driving.

I had just finished my drink when I saw him. A small boy, tan and curly-haired, wearing a raggedy T-shirt and shorts, entered the open doorway and looked around. He looked as though he hadn't eaten in a week. As he approached me, I reached into my pocket to give him a little something.

"Are you looking for Max?" He spoke with a heavy Spanish accent.

I smiled. "Word gets around."

"I can take you to him."

"He send you to find me?"

The boy pulled at my arm, so I nodded and stood up.

"Where is he?"

"You come with me."

We went out into the light of the afternoon and headed down a street. The boy looked earnest enough to be legit, but I didn't understand what the big deal was. I assumed I would find Max in a local watering hole, drunk enough to welcome me with open arms. After checking four bars and coming up with nothing, I had started wondering if Max was even around.

"How do you know Max?" I asked the kid who kept tugging at my shirt as he hurried down the street.

"I know everyone."

"What's your name?"

"Armando," the boy said in an earnest tone. "I have lived here all my life."

"Good place to be born."

"I like the ocean."

"Yeah, me too. I was born in Knoxville, Tennessee. Ever heard of that?"

The boy shook his head.

"How about Chicago? That's where I live."

"I see pictures of Chicago. Big city."

I nodded as we started walking down an alley that ran between a shop and a hotel.

"Is Max meeting us?" I asked Armando.

"Yes. Just down here."

The heat of the day and the ache of the travel on the steamship from the mainland and the soreness from my near-death experience in Chicago had made me tired. More tired than usual. More tired and less on my guard. But I was in Key West. Who could possibly be looking for me down here? But this fatigue and the sun shining down in my eyes and the hand of the little boy leading me down the alley all made me miss the man who came out of nowhere and hit me over the head.

All I could do was shove Armando out of the way, as if the little boy were in danger.

As if the little boy hadn't led me right to the assailant.

My eyes took a long time to open. They were heavy, and lifting my eyelids took work. A small light shone from somewhere behind me, but I couldn't see the source. I was sitting in a chair with my hands and feet tied together. And tied well. I opened and shut my eyes to get a clearer idea of my surroundings.

I was sitting in a warehouse that appeared empty. Echoes of noise sounded around me. I looked on each side but saw nothing.

I jumped when the barrel of a gun jammed into my forehead.

"You a friend of Maxie the Frenchman?"

That was a new title, I thought. Maxie the Frenchman. Good ole Max must've really done something this time.

"An acquaintance. That's all."

"What do you want with him?"

"Can I ask why I'm tied up, and why you're pointing a gun at my head?"

The man walked around in front of me. He was short and had a beard on an otherwise hair-free head. He held the gun at his side.

"What is a nice young man like you doing looking for filth like Maxie?"

The stranger had a thick accent, possibly Cuban. He was dark-skinned, like the boy who had led me here.

"Where is Armando?"

"Don't worry about him. Worry about yourself."

"I'm guessing he is your son."

The man laughed. "I'm many things, but a father I'm not."

"There's no need for guns here."

"There's always a need for guns. What's your name?"

"Henry."

"So, Henry. Do you have any children?"

I shook my head. The man with the gun was pacing in front of me. It sounded like someone else might be behind me.

"I'm guessing you're not related to our friend Max, right?"

"Just a former colleague. A student of his."

"A student? Max is a teacher?"

"Why am I tied up?"

The man stopped pacing and stood right in front of me, looking down. "To make sure you would stay put."

"I'm not going anywhere."

"If you're anything like Max, you have a tendency to show up in the wrong places, then to disappear in the right ones."

"I'm not like Max, and I don't like being threatened."

"What is your business with Max?"

"Visiting a friend. That's all."

He looked at me for a moment.

"You wouldn't be looking for Salvador, would you?"

The name meant nothing to me. "I have no idea who that is," I said.

"Max knows. So when you find him, tell him that Salvador is looking for him."

"Who says Max is even around?"

"He's around. So you tell him. Tell him that Salvador's looking for him. Tell him that you met me, that I'm keeping an eye out on you, a very close eye. Got that?"

I nodded, but I didn't understand what any of this was about.

Except that it involved Max, which could mean anything.

In the end, it wasn't difficult finding Max. I knew it would be in a bar. I just didn't realize he had picked up a new hobby.

"Deal 'em," I heard the familiar voice say to the smoky room in the back of the tavern.

"I don't see any more money."

"Trust me, there is money to be made."

"You already owe ten thousand."

"We're all gentlemen here, correct?" Max asked just as I stepped through the door.

Four heads turned to look at me.

Max looked the same as ever, a little more tanned, his gray hair still short, a wry grin hanging off his long and lean face.

"What do you want?" asked a man with a pile of cash in front of him.

I recognized the voice as the one who'd been reminding Max of his indebtedness a moment before.

"Someone said this is where I could find a good poker game."

"Game's over," he said.

Max didn't say a word, just sat and smiled and stared. He had nothing but a very full ashtray on the table in front of him.

"Come on—it doesn't look over," I said. "There have to be a few hands left to play."

Another guy, fidgety with eyes roaming everywhere, sat and smoked a cigarette.

"Mister, we're fine, thanks," said the first man.

"Roy, let the man play a few hands." It was the fourth man speaking, a redhead with pale eyebrows and paler skin.

I nodded at Max. He gave no sign of recognition.

Roy scratched a thick day's worth of beard. "I only play when I see cash."

I took out the wad of bills I'd been carrying around in my pocket since getting off the boat. I plunked it down on the table, glad to be rid of the burden of possibly losing it. The men looked up at me. I had their full attention.

With a meaty hand wiping the sweaty skin of his neck, Roy nodded. "You want to give money away, fine with me. Grab his chair."

"No, no," Max said. "I'm staying." He produced a hundred-dollar bill for ante.

"Where'd you get that?" Roy said.

"I told you, I'm good for it."

"You're good for nothing."

I pulled up a chair and sat next to Max. He reached out to shake my hand.

"Max Joubert," he said, emphasizing the French last name.

"Henry Wolfe," I said.

He gripped my hand tightly, making me wince.

"It's my pleasure," he said, then winked.

An hour later, a pivotal hand was underway.

The group had weaned two already: the redhead, who went four hands and busted, and Max, who already owed his right arm to Roy and now just sat downing drinks he didn't have money to pay for and talking way too much.

My money had quadrupled, while Roy had gone on a long losing streak. We were playing straight poker, one hundred dollars minimum.

I got the first card. It was the jack of hearts. Next was a four of diamonds. Then another jack. Then an ace. Then a jack.

I can play poker. My expression always stays the same. Most of the time I'm not horribly worried about winning or losing, and this day was no different.

Roy was a decent player. But he hated losing. I could tell he was the big man around here, the one everybody let talk and win. He sat there sweating, jaw clenched, surely wishing he hadn't let me sit in, surely believing he would win his money back. It wasn't his looks that gave him away. It was his actions. The more movement he made when he got new cards, the better his hand. They were slight, subtle movements, but I noticed.

After this hand was dealt, he was still. Still as a dead person.

"I'll raise you five hundred," he said.

I had already made five or six thousand, while Max had revealed he owed Roy around seven. My hope was to make a clean slate for my old friend. I hadn't figured out how exactly to do this. Maybe I would simply take my earnings and then give them to Max later. It could be that easy, right?

I studied my cards. Every third hand I would rub my face, as if studying something. Every sixth hand I'd let out a deep sigh. I'd recount after the exhale, doing the same thing once again. Max always laughed at my antics. But they were working. Roy had no idea what each gesture or sound meant.

This was the sixth hand again, so I let out the seemingly frustrated breath.

"I'll see you and raise you two thousand."

Roy looked up at me, surprised. I hadn't raised much tonight, except for one time when it was obvious I was bluffing.

Max laughed. "What will you do, Roy? Biggest raise of the night."

Roy smoked a cigarette and thought. He had nothing, I knew that, but he thought I didn't either.

"I think it's the biggest bluff of the night," he said. He took a drag. "Henry, right?"

I nodded.

"I've never seen you around here before."

"Just got in."

"From where?"

"Oh, around. Last up in New York."

"You don't sound like a New Yorker."

"I'm from a little of everywhere."

"And what brings you to Key West?"

"I'm visiting an old friend."

"Old?" Max blurted out.

Obviously the man had spent time around Max, especially inebriated Max, who might say anything. He ignored my friend's remark.

"So you probably don't know who I am," Roy said.

"Does this have anything to do with the game?"

He took another drag. "I don't like cheaters."

"You're a sore loser, Roy," Max said. "How can he be cheating? He's not even dealing."

"I find your timing interesting," he told me.

"I find yours pretty slow," I replied, nodding my head and aiming my eyes at his cards.

The other men watching around the table chuckled. Roy jerked his head at one of them, then the other, his face turning red.

"I'll match and raise you another thousand."

The pot was close to ten thousand.

"I'll call," I said.

"What do you have?"

I placed my cards on the table without saying anything. There was a low grunt from one of the men. Roy just looked at the cards for a long time, then stared at me, his teeth clenched and eyes burning over. Max started laughing.

I took the money and looked over at Max, who was shaking his head as if to say *Well, you did it now, didn't you?*

"Another hand?" I asked, the smile escaping on my lips impossible to contain.

Roy opened his mouth, then bit his lip and shook his head. He stood up, looking at Max. "I want my money. Now."

Max nodded. "I don't have it here."

The man's eyes narrowed, small slits through which he eyed his options.

"I want it. Tonight. Lloyd, get James and follow Max back to his hotel room. And as for you—Henry, is it?"

I nodded as I stacked the wad of bills.

"I'd suggest that you leave as quickly as you got here. I don't make many mistakes, and I sure don't like being reminded of them."

Roy didn't give me time to respond. He paced out of the room, and I could tell he was a man not used to rushing or worrying. Those in life who rush do so for a reason, and Roy didn't have to. He also was not used to turning his back on failure, especially his own.

Max stood up and looked at me. He winked, a habit that seemed to reflect the very essence of the man standing there. It said a lot of things—mostly, for now, that he would be okay.

He walked out with the two men following him, leaving me with a mass of money I hadn't even wanted to win.

I heard the footsteps behind me. I didn't need to turn to see who it was.

"It took you long enough," I said.

"I was a bit delayed."

The French accent was still there, of course, but years of living in America and abroad had toned it down. Max walked past my table and pulled up a chair across from me. Music still played in the street, though it was close to midnight.

"Wonderful weather, wouldn't you say?"

I nodded. "Have any trouble with those goons?"

"No. No trouble at all."

He looked around for a waiter.

"I think they are gone for the night."

"Ah, yes, 'tis my tardiness." He produced a small black flask, barely visible in the muted light of the street. "Care for a sip?"

"I'm good." I watched him. "What are you doing in Key West, Max?"

"What are *you* doing in Key West?"

"Looking for you."

"I'm found."

"What have you been up to?"

"Let me see. . . . Come to think of it, this paints the picture pretty well."

He took another sip. I could tell from his voice and his eyes that he was drunk.

"You know, that'll eventually catch up with you," I told him.

"So will Roy."

"He's harmless."

Max laughed. "You not only insulted him, you took his money."

"Isn't that what poker is all about?"

"Not with Roy. You don't know him."

"So you deliberately lose?"

Max shook his head. "No, I'm just eternally unlucky with cards. I never win. But that doesn't mean I shouldn't try."

"That makes a lot of sense," I said. "Oh, and by the way, Salvador says hi."

Max stiffened a bit in his chair, his eyes on mine.

"Yeah, one of his men said it with a gun pointed at my head and a rope tied around my hands," I continued.

"When was this?"

"Oh, earlier in the day."

"Is he following you?"

"Probably," I said. "I'm not sure. Care to divulge?"

Max took another drink, this one a little longer than the others. "Maybe another time."

"I get a gun to the head, and you get to say 'another time.'"

"I didn't bring you down here. I'm guessing it wasn't for midnight conversation."

"Max—I've got a proposition for you."

"Let me guess." He beamed a smile, the wrinkles around his eyes making him look more mischievous than wise.

"Sure."

"Trip to Brazil," he said. "Deep in the jungle. Looking for a lost adventurer. The fountain of youth. Et cetera, et cetera."

"Who told you?"

"Someone obviously didn't tell you."

"Tell me what?" I asked.

"That they already asked me. That I said no. So they sent you down to come ask me. Again."

"Who are *they*?"

"I imagine it was Arthur who sent you, right?"

I nodded.

"Ah, dear Arthur. He didn't make the trip to Key West. I so desperately wanted to see him come, all pale and sick from being on a boat. Instead, some other idiot came down."

"I told Arthur it was going to be impossible."

Max laughed. "Yeah, well, a few things have changed since I told them no."

"Like?"

He scratched his nose, then took another drink. "Just . . . things."

"What does that mean?"

"You know, you look good, Henry."

"Wish I could say the same about you."

"I'm alive, right?"

"You have that knack. You might not be good at cards, but you are good at staying alive."

"Seems I've taught you well, then."

"You heard about Chicago?" I asked.

"This isn't the jungle. I hear things."

"Don't believe everything you hear."

He nodded. "So what's your take on this whole thing?"

"The expedition? Sounds interesting. I need to go on another adventure. You know how I hate the daily grind."

"Me too," Max said.

We watched a couple pass, arm in arm, young lovers out for a stroll. I looked at Max.

"Max, I'm sorry. . . ."

"Yes, we're all sorry."

"If I could have—"

"Henry?"

"Yes?"

"I'll agree to go with you on this expedition. It's fine." He shook his head, looking exhausted, then looked around to see if anyone was nearby. "Just—you must promise me one thing. No mentioning her name. Not once. Never. I hear it, I walk. You understand?"

This was the first glimpse of the Max I'd assumed I would find. There was anger deep down, but more than that, there was hurt.

I nodded.

"That and—well—whatever they agreed to pay you, I want it doubled. I'll take some of your money. You don't need more anyway."

He laughed, and his laugh reminded me of a hundred other laughs and memories. It was good to hear.

The coffee was stronger than I was accustomed to. I took small sips, the bitterness sharp and biting. I was sitting in the lobby of the aged hotel in which Max had been living, having checked out of my room. Everything here looked faded by the sun—once vibrant reds and oranges looked washed over, the sheen and polish dulled, dust and sand locked in corners. The bright squinting glow of morning filled the room.

It was twenty minutes past the time Max and I were supposed to meet, and I was wondering if I should go upstairs and get him. Our ship left in less than an hour. It was the only one for the day.

I finished the last sip of coffee like it was a shot of tequila, and just as I put the cup down on the table, the door opened and two men walked in. I was sitting close to the windows, the sun bright at my back, so the men didn't see me as they strode right toward the stairs. One of them held a pistol.

Once they were out of sight, I jumped up, looking for something to help out with. I never carried a gun, and used one only if I had to. I was better at running. I thought for a second.

As I was about to go looking for the hotel manager, who seemed conveniently absent at the moment, I heard a couple of shots. Then a series of more shots. Not from a handgun, but from a tommy gun. They were violent, relentless.

I froze, my body numb. Max. Poor Max. He had angered one too many people.

I breathed in and out. My suitcase was on the floor next to me. I picked it up and thought again.

I couldn't do a thing for Max. I couldn't go up there, I had no gun, I couldn't—

I knew I could get out of there and try and find some help. Any help.

The tommy gun roared again. Sweat filled the back of my neck. My throat felt dry and hard.

Poor Max. This man and mentor and father figure and figure that passed by outside the window on the street in front of the hotel.

Max?

I bolted toward the open doorway and called out his name.

"You're alive!" he cried out.

He was breathless and pale, though probably not as pale as I was.

"*I'm* alive? What—did you hear that?"

"Yes. Now that is a way to wake up."

"What do you mean—it woke you up? How'd you get out of there?"

"I jumped," Max said, wearing a button-down shirt not buttoned and pants not belted. "Nearly killed myself, too. These fifty-four-year-old legs aren't what they used to be."

I had a strange sense of complete confusion. Max often brought this on.

"Aren't you hurt? Shot?"

"Shot? No. Why would I be?"

I raised my hands. "Uh, the guns? The men?"

"They broke down *your* door. Right next to mine."

"Let's get out of here," I said, starting to jog down the road. "I thought they killed you."

"And I thought they killed you."

"Me? What'd I do?"

"Like I said—you don't take Roy's money. And you never, never insult him."

"*Now* you tell me," I called over my shoulder.

"Next time tell me you're coming."

"Next time leave me an address where I can find you."

"That boat leaving soon?"

"Not soon enough."

ON BOARD THE *STARCROSSER*

January 17, 1929

Someone's watching us."

Max looked up from his newspaper. "You just noticed?"

"What's that supposed to mean?"

"I've read this paper three times now, all the way through," he said, standing up from the chair on the outside deck of the steamer we had been on for three days. "I hate ships. Nothing but sea for miles. Nothing to do."

"Who do you think it is?"

Max walked over to the railing. He squinted as he looked up. His bare arms were lean and muscular in the short-sleeved shirt he wore.

"You have many enemies, Henry?"

I stood beside him staring out at the ocean. It was a hypnotizing sight, easy to doze off looking at. There was a nice breeze on this clear day.

I told him I wasn't sure.

"No, listen. I'm not talking about people who can't stand your writing. Those fluff articles you do for magazines or that outrageous book you wrote. I'm talking about people who'd get on a ship from Miami heading to Rio just to keep an eye on you."

"You have such a gentle way with words."

He ignored my comment. "Think—this could be important. Life or death."

"I've been nearly killed two times in the same amount of months," I said. "Life or death has been the theme recently."

Of course Bugs Moran wanted me dead, but as long as I was out of Chicago and out of the public writing arena, he wouldn't be chasing after me. I tried to think of who else might want me dead that badly, but nobody came to mind.

"Same here," Max said. "I can think of plenty of people who might like to toss me over this rail and wave good-bye as I bobbed up and down in the salty waters below. But they're not going to follow me all the way to South America. I doubt either one of us will be vacationing in Key West again—but those fellows aren't going to spy on us."

"So who do you think he is, then?"

" 'He'?"

"Yeah," I said. "The dark-haired guy, mustache."

"I count three myself."

"Three? Were you going to fill me in at any point?"

"Possibly. But, Henry, you have this way about you."

"What kind of way is that?"

His expression was reflective, controlled, slightly above-it-all even when he didn't mean for it to be. "Sometimes the drama you so love to write about follows you around in a very loud and public way."

"That's not true."

"That was the first time I've heard a tommy gun in a long time. It's as if they knew the great Henry Wolfe was around. Time to get out the big guns."

I laughed. "Please."

"The only thing I can guess is that it has something to do with this expedition."

"Like what?"

"They really wanted us along for this trip, didn't they? To find a missing group of explorers."

"The Prescott family is wealthy."

Max nodded. "I don't think these men are attached to the Prescotts. Maybe someone doesn't want Louis Prescott found."

"Or the lost city—the Devil's Mouth."

"Or there's one other possibility."

"What's that?"

"Those men—they might be working for our German friend."

"Richter?" I asked. "He doesn't want us dead."

"Of course not. But he'd leave us for dead if there were treasure involved. And, if you remember, we didn't exactly part on the best of terms."

I recalled seeing Richter being escorted away at gunpoint as Max and I left the desert in a stolen truck. *His* stolen truck.

"Do you think he made it out of Egypt alive?"

Max nodded. "Maybe he just didn't like the way you portrayed him in your book."

"Maybe he wants to find this 'Devil's Mouth' first."

Max looked at me and flashed his remarkably straight, white teeth. "These tall tales—lost cities, devils, eternal youth. They're the stuff of legend, of adventurers selling something. They never turn out to be real."

"What we found in Egypt. That was real."

"That, my friend, was a fluke. Put enough random events in a random place in a random universe together, and anything can happen."

"Max. You know that's not true."

"The only true thing I know is what I see here, right now. That we're on a ship with very bad food and cheap liquor bound for something we're not going to find because it's not there."

"Those men following us—they're real."

"Did you bring a gun?"

I laughed. "Of course not."

"When we get back to the room, I'll give you my extra."

"Max—no."

"It's hard enough to watch my own back," he said. "I can't keep watching yours."

Max still had the appetite of a horse. He wanted to have an early dinner, so I told him I'd meet him up on the dining room level. I wanted to change my shirt, soaked from sitting in the sun all afternoon. It was evening now, and the light was falling toward the west.

As I rounded the passageway, narrow and dimly lit, I noticed the door to my stateroom partially opened.

"Max, I thought you said you were—"

I stopped at the doorway as I looked down at a dark-skinned man rummaging through my opened suitcase on the bed, clothes tossed to the side.

"Hey!"

I started toward the man, but he rushed right at me. He was short, but wiry and strong, and slammed me with his hands against the wall. I howled out in pain, then scrambled to my feet. There wasn't time to see if he'd taken anything valuable. I raced after the man as he bolted down the hallway.

He took the stairs heading up. I hit the same stairs and slipped, falling on a knee and slicing it open. I could see the doorway to the deck above open.

I reached the deck and saw my assailant sprinting to the right. He plowed into an elegantly dressed couple, doubtless headed for dinner, as if they were bowling pins. The man in the top hat and cane remained sprawled out on the ground, while his wife quickly stood and picked up his cane.

"Sorry about that," I told them as I ran past.

I felt a hard thwack on my back and didn't want to stop to ask the woman why. Chances were she'd take another crack, possibly to the head.

The man found another set of stairs and took them two at a time. I did the same, but not as quickly. You would think that a man who does so much running in his life—running away, that is—would be better at it, but the stranger I was following was fast.

Thankfully, there were blockades in his sprint.

A waiter suddenly found his tray shoved against his face as the man crashed into him.

I doubted the waiter would pummel me as had the woman seconds ago, but I didn't want to take a chance, so I didn't bother even looking his way.

We rushed through a doorway, then another, then through the main dining hall. I heard a scream, then breaking glass. I tried to avoid a waitress with three plates but just grazed her, sending everything toppling. Just as I ran past a table, something clipped my leg and sent me flying. I fell next to another table, landing on my back, rolling around like an infant only to sit up and try to get my bearings. A slender blonde in a deep blue dress stared down at me like I was the morning trash.

"Above everything, don't get the fish," I told her as I stood up and continued sprinting.

There was another howl, a yell, a crash. The thief was having a hard go of it himself. He wasn't far away.

I saw him reach a doorway out of the dining room, thankfully, and I followed, past it and onto another set of stairs. There were sure lots of stairs around here. We finally reached the sun deck, now bathed in the orange glow of sunset.

On the wooden deck, mostly empty now that it was dusk, I kicked it into high gear. The man hesitated, as though trying to decide which way to go. This was his error. I raced and caught up with him. He was winded, I could see, and confused as well. Evading someone had probably not been in the plans.

I seized the back of his shirt, pulling it hard, and jerked him down. Then I rammed a knee down on his gut and squeezed his bony neck.

For a second, I caught my breath. A couple walked past, and I nodded at them. "Beautiful evening, isn't it?" I asked as the man underneath me groaned.

I looked back at him. "Okay, buddy, what'd you take?"

The man looked frightened and young—he was eighteen or twenty years old, if that. He also looked as though he didn't understand a word I had said.

"Come on—what'd you take?"

I searched him—he weighed less than I did, so it was easy to hold him down.

"What's your name? Why are you snooping in my room? Huh?"

He blurted out something that sounded Portuguese.

"Let me guess," I said. "You don't understand English."

I patted down his legs and found something in one of his pant pockets.

"Take it out," I said, pointing at his pocket, then grabbing his neck again and tightening my grip to make sure he knew I was serious.

He took out a folded-up paper that turned out to be a map. I looked at it.

"Where'd you get this?"

The man just stared at me.

The map looked unfamiliar, its folds and creases aged with faint notations and markings.

I held it in front of his eyes. "What'd you want with this? Where'd you get this?"

"My suitcase," a familiar voice called out from behind.

I looked around to see Max.

"What is this?" I asked, annoyed and borderline angry.

He laughed. "I was only saving us a table for two. You didn't tell me we'd have guests."

"I didn't know I'd find him in our rooms going through our stuff."

"And I thought you were just playing tag."

"What is this, Max?" I asked again.

"That is a map."

"Yeah, I know that. But of what?"

"Come on—let's take this man to the crew. I'll tell you about the map later."

"Anything else you want to share?"

He looked at my sweaty forehead and grinned. "You need a bath."

We brought the man to the lieutenant's office. They were going to hold him until we reached Rio. So far he hadn't said a word; he didn't relent even when a couple of the crew spoke to him in other languages.

At dinner, as I sat and picked at food I didn't want, I waited for Max to reveal yet another secret to me.

He didn't used to keep so many things from me.

"I've taken a lot of trips, Henry. Not every adventure has been with you."

"I know that. You were already a legend when I took your class."

Max balked at that. "Legend? Please. What exactly is your definition of a legend? You probably have to die to truly become legendary, and you know, I'd prefer to stay alive."

"You know what I mean."

"Ten years ago or thereabouts I took a group down to Brazil to find a lost city in the wilderness. There it is again—the legendary lost city. If something is lost, why do so many people want to find it? But I was leading the group, determined to do what no other had."

"You never told me about that," I said.

"Don't look wounded, my boy. You never asked."

I nodded. Max looked much better than he had when I had first met up with him in Key West. Being in debt to people and worrying about being killed at any given point of the day can really do a number on a man's looks. He looked rested and healthier, though I could see he was still drinking too much.

"Henry, we got close—so very close—to something. This Devil's Mouth—I heard rumors of such a place. A place men sought in pursuit of unlimited riches and immortality—but in fact was impossible to reach, and led only to death. A cursed place."

"Was it true?"

"I don't know. My men were killed by Indians."

"I thought most of the Indians in those areas were friendly," I said.

"Not really. The farther in you go, the more likely it is to reach tribes who have never seen white men. Tribes who might not necessarily be dangerous, but are simply protecting what they know. We're invaders to them; this is their land. It was almost as if we got too close. The men on our expedition became fearful. Gravely fearful, of devils and ghosts."

"And you were the only one to survive?" I asked.

He drained his drink. "Yes. And barely survive. A friendly local tribe nursed me back to health and brought me to a nearby town."

"So do you believe there's a lost city waiting to be found?"

Max looked at me, his face serious, devoid of its usual good humor. "There is something. Something that people don't want found. Something that a lot have tried to get to."

He held up the map.

"I got close. Ten years ago, I got close. And I made a vow to myself that one day, I'd try to go back."

The Atlantic sounded wild. The ship swayed a little more than usual. Thankfully I'd always had a good set of sea legs. But the rolling did prevent me from sleeping. I got up from my room and went next door. The door was partially opened, but this time I found the appropriate proprietor inside.

Max sat in a chair, smoking a cigarette. "Care to join me?"

"Why not?"

We sat in the small room, smoking and looking around in the muted light.

Eventually Max broke the silence. "I'm surprised you haven't settled down," he said.

"I have you as a role model."

"Hmm." He nodded. "You'll soon be at an age where you can't blame your elders. There will be no one around to point at."

"Maybe some men aren't born to settle down."

"So they're born to what? Ride the waves? Hunt and explore? Sit around fires at night and sweat in the hot jungle by day?"

"Yeah, something like that." I took a drag from the cigarette.

"Men don't explore because they're brave. It's because they're scared. They don't want to deal with what's happening on the home front, so they run into the woods and the wild. They run and keep running. And when they end up dead, they're appointed heroes."

"You're certainly optimistic tonight."

"I hate these steamers. You're cooped up and fighting nausea. All you can do is sit around and think about how cooped up you are."

"I see you're getting into the spirit of Rio."

"I'm getting it out of my system, my young man. Because once you go into those jungles, your body starts to shut down on you. I figure to have a little more fun before the pain comes."

"There's still some time in Rio for that," I said.

"I know that too."

"So why'd you end up in Key West?" I asked.

Kind eyes stared back at me, as did a congenial glance. "The sun. The fish. The slow pace. What would you like me to say?"

"The truth."

"Same reason I'm on this boat. Running away, my boy. Running."

I remained silent for a long time, then finally ventured to speak. "It was nobody's fault, what happened in Africa."

I would do what I promised—I wouldn't mention her name.

"Oh, come on, Henry. For a while I blamed myself, then that got tiring so I blamed you, and that didn't work because it certainly wasn't your fault. Then I blamed God, but he wasn't talking back to me. So I stopped blaming."

"And you ran to Key West?"

Max nodded and smiled. "It's better brooding when the sun beams down on you. I've had enough Chicago winters to last a life-time."

"I'm sorry," I said.

"Of course you are. We all are. I thought I had it, Henry. I really thought I had it. Love. A life. A chance to settle down, little Maxies running around. But fate had a way of dealing with us, didn't it?"

"We're lucky to have gotten out of there alive."

"Lucky?" Max laughed and flicked his cigarette butt away. "I don't know if I believe in luck, my boy. Was it luck that we managed to get out of Key West today?"

"I'd say so."

"Remember what that woman told you? In the little village? You ever think about that?"

I nodded, looking away.

Max continued. "I heard what she said. To both of us. And Kalila wasn't so fortunate. The woman didn't say anything about Kalila, and she died."

"That old woman was just trying to make a little money," I said.

"Yes, but we got out alive, didn't we?"

"We did everything we should have and got lucky."

My older friend shook his head. "It wasn't our time. I had not yet encountered the river of black that she talked about."

"And what happens when you do?"

"Then we see who will win. Destiny or the gods or one God or random luck. So be it."

Max looked around the ground and found a small tin cup. He poured me a drink, then held up the bottle.

"To my long lost friend, Henry. Cheers to fate, destiny, and the black rivers where we'll all meet our demise."

RIO DE JANEIRO

The steamer arrived in Rio midmorning, and from the deck I took in the sights as the boat passed the city and headed to Guanabara Bay to the municipal docks. I could see the famous Copacabana Beach and Palace Hotel, the massive rock hill called Sugarloaf Mountain that resembled a thumb sticking out of the ground, the Corcovado and the large statue of Christ that was being built. I had never been to Rio before, having gotten closest when I stayed in the northern city of Salvador for a few weeks. The air smelled of adventure and aspiration. For a moment I thought of waking Max, but I didn't want his hangover to spoil my mood.

He appeared soon enough, looking remarkably composed for someone so incoherent just hours earlier. I could tell the city didn't give him goose bumps like it did me, but I saw an eager glint in his eyes.

We took a taxi down the busy Rio Branco Avenue, and I listened to Max detail some of his experiences in the city, of meeting some young local lady before leaving and never seeing her again, of learning how to do something he called the *samba*, of heading to the royal city of Petropolis fifty miles out of Rio.

I found myself so lost in his stories and in the surroundings that I didn't say anything as we rode to the hotel.

"A conversation is something that's held between people," Max said.

"I'm just listening. And enjoying myself."

Max wiped his forehead. "Do you know this happens to be their summer?"

"Really? I couldn't tell," I replied.

"Do you know what Rio de Janeiro means?"

I shook my head.

"Didn't you ever pay attention in class?"

"I paid attention to Emily Hutchinson."

Max nodded. "Yes. I think I paid attention to her too. *Rio de Janeiro* is Portuguese for 'river of January.' I guess the original explorers assumed that Guanabara Bay was the mouth of a river. Here in Brazil, Rio is known as the *Cidade Maravilhosa*, the Marvelous City."

"I liked your personal anecdotes better than the history lesson."

"I've always thought of Rio as the middle ground of grand exploration. In front of you, you have the wild and raging Atlantic Ocean, while behind you sits the uncharted wilderness of the Brazilian highlands. Anywhere you go you're apt to find adventure."

"Then we've come to the right place," I said, watching a group of well-dressed men and women strolling down the street looking in windows.

"It's a pity more people don't get a chance to see the rest of the world. It opens your eyes, doesn't it? Shows that there's more than just a little house on a little corner of a little town."

"Some people like that little house on a little corner."

Max nodded. "But they close their eyes to the reality that there is more, that there is *this*." He waved toward the street outside the window. "They claim to have all the answers, but the more you discover, the more questions you have. A lot of people in this world never even get off the boat."

To describe Kate Prescott's sweeping into my life will surely do injustice to the moment I first beheld this glorious woman. I will attempt it nonetheless. But realize that she's not by my side as I write this, or resting in a room nearby, or waiting down the street waiting to meet up. This is not a love story. Oh, maybe it is in some ways. Love is a word that can be used in many ways. But this is not the story of boy meets girl, boy loses girl, boy wins girl in the end. It is, however, where a grown-up boy meets a grown-up girl in the wild romantic air of Rio.

It was my first night in Rio, and to be rid of the boat and the endless sea was a relief. I don't get seasick, but I do get sick of the sea. The endless blues and greens and grays and the endless amount of walking and resting and waiting. I read and write a lot on a ship, but that's not what I love doing. I love *doing*, simple as that. Doing anything. So in the great city of Brazil, bookended by the great ocean on one side and the great mountainous jungle on the other, Rio offered relief. It also offered the chance to finally see whom we would be traveling with on this expedition.

Arthur Holden, and Max for that matter, had neglected to mention her. The fact that there was a *her* to mention shocked and surprised me.

We had agreed to meet at the restaurant in the hotel, an older hotel with excellent service and quality. The restaurant itself was small—it couldn't have held more than thirty people. Our table was in the center of the room and could have accommodated a dozen people.

Max and I were welcomed by a short, smiling man with a graying beard. Shaking his hand, I knew it was Colonel Cuaron.

"Henry Wolfe," I said to him. "I've heard many good things about you, Colonel."

He nodded and shook hands with Max, then tried to repeat Max's full name.

"Max Joobah?"

"Close enough," Max said.

"It is an honor," the Colonel said.

"Please, no such thing."

"Were your travels well?"

"Yes. But very glad to see land."

I realized with some bit of irony I was the only person here speaking English without a foreign accent.

Glancing around the room, I noticed a broad-shouldered

Brazilian standing by the side of the table. He looked physically incapable of smiling.

"This is Mateo, one of my men. He will be coming along on the trip."

We shook hands, and I guessed Mateo could rip me apart with one of his. I was taller, but his muscles made him look bigger.

"You'll meet some of my men tonight. Most do not speak English. Mateo does not. But he is very loyal to me and a very good man for our trip."

Mateo excused himself. I wasn't sure if it was the Colonel's wish or it was a cultural thing. Or if the man simply didn't want to sit at a table all evening listening to foreign conversation.

The Colonel offered us a local drink, and we settled down to listen to his descriptions and history of the hotel.

I liked Colonel Cuaron. He had a sophisticated air about him, an air men like Max and me had thrown overboard years ago. But he liked to laugh. Anybody who enjoys laughing can't be all bad. His eyes gave away his heart—full and overflowing. And inside it was a radiant light he liked to share.

His dark green eyes seemed tinted with gold as they watched me. "You are a writer?" he asked.

"Yes. Sometimes."

"A famous writer?"

"Yes, famous in his head," Max called out from across the table. "He gets his best material from me."

"Have you been to South America before?"

"Several times," I said. "It's a beautiful place."

I started to detail my last visit here with great enthusiasm.

Sometimes telling a story simply works. You have a captive and interested audience, and you can sense that the words you say will remain in the memories of your listeners for days and weeks to come. I was in midsentence when the doors to the restaurant were flung open, and a woman's loud, excited voice interrupted my own.

All of our heads turned. And in strolled Kate. Confident, loud, busy Kate.

If only I could go back to relive it all over again, I would. In a heartbeat.

I told you we were at the wrong hotel! This is not a good sign! We could have been there all night. You need to listen to me! Hi, I'm Kate."

The golden brown hair stood out, long and wild and windswept. Everything about Kate, in my initial glance, looked—strong. Strong eyes, with a vibrant teal color that didn't back down. Strong jawline. Strong, full lips that coiled into a smile at the men standing to shake hands with her.

I looked at Max, then at the Colonel, and neither of them seemed surprised at the woman talking to them. I wanted to know what I was missing.

She wore a white dress with buttons down the front and held her hat in one hand. She was tall and tan.

"I'm so sorry we're late. This is Anton, our guide. He 'guided' me to the wrong place."

The tall blond man next to her shook my hand and seemed unfazed by the woman's remarks.

Colonel Cuaron knew the land better than anybody, and in many ways he was the designated leader of our group. But I learned that Anton was the guide the Prescott family had sent. My first guess was that he was Swedish.

I still had no idea why this woman named Kate was joining us. That's what beauty can do to a man.

My eyes stayed on her. She found her way to me.

"Henry Wolfe," she said, a grin on her lips as if there was a story behind the name. "I'm so glad you were able to make it."

Her grip was strong, her attention fleeting. I was about to say something but she was already shaking Max's hand.

"You are lovelier than your picture shows," Max said.

"My picture? What picture might that be?"

"I read magazines. I've seen you with your family."

And then it made sense. This was Kate Prescott, the daughter of the Prescott family who was paying for this expedition, the sister of the missing explorer we were looking for, the socialite that I had read about but temporarily forgotten.

I looked at Max and wondered why I was the last to know everything.

"Kate is leading this expedition," he told me.

I opened my mouth to say something, but couldn't. The words escaped me.

"They didn't tell you?" Kate asked me in genuine surprise. "I must confess, it was a last-minute decision for me to come."

I only nodded. Kate glanced at me, and the look in her eye—was it actually what I saw?

She was amused. Amused at my being so taken aback by her

being here that I couldn't think of anything to say.

"I felt this expedition needed a little more of a feminine touch," she said, the glimmer in her eyes still there.

I looked away, curious, caught completely off guard.

And also annoyed that Max had neglected to tell me about Kate coming along for the journey. Or that she was completely breathtaking.

I noticed her playfully sparring tone. I was going to say something, but once again I found I couldn't speak. And that startled me even more than Kate's glance.

Typically quick with a witty comeback, I couldn't say a word.

Max just laughed and slapped me on the back. "He's been traveling for several days," he said, as if I were deaf. "He's a little overwhelmed, like the rest of us, to see a woman of such beauty who's not a local, but from our beloved States."

Kate laughed. "Perhaps Henry could speak for himself next time. The real beauties are just outside. Ah, to have been born in South America. Dark Amazonian beauties."

"Yes," Colonel Cuaron said, adding, "but you fit in with the rest of them. Just a little more fair-skinned."

She smiled at him. "I am starving. Colonel, please tell me you've ordered one of everything."

"I can do that."

"Please do. I'm sure Henry and Max are hungry, and I can probably eat as much as both of them. But that wouldn't be very ladylike, would it?"

Kate sat down in the chair next to mine. A waiter came to ask what she wanted to drink, and she ordered a lemonade without hesitation.

Several other men filed in, a couple from the Colonel's group, a few others with Kate. She had come to Rio with a large group, even though not all of them were coming on the expedition.

I watched her for a while as she spoke with Colonel Cuaron about the city. She eventually noticed me staring.

"Mr. Wolfe—I'd say the cat has got your tongue."

"No, not a cat," I said, finally feeling more myself. "More like a tiger."

She raised her eyebrows. "You're an observant man. But I wouldn't say tiger. I'd say a snow leopard."

This surprised me, and I wondered if it was just a random comment.

She smiled. "Max isn't the only one around here who reads."

I was impressed. She knew more about me than I realized. And it wasn't just the book, either.

I grinned and nodded.

This was going to be very interesting.

So, Mr. Wolfe, tell me about yourself."

"What would you like to know besides the fact that my name is Henry?" I asked. "You already know that I hope to see a snow leopard in person one day, an obscure fact from some newspaper interview awhile ago."

So far Kate had talked about their trip here from New York, the food on the ship, the fact that she couldn't eat spicy foods, their first night in Rio, and several other rambling details related to a story that I didn't necessarily catch. I was surprised she was letting me talk.

"What *should* I know?" Kate asked.

"He has a weakness for beautiful women," Max chimed in, always the socialite, working several conversations at once.

"I learned from a master," I said.

"I'm his mentor."

I looked at Max, then at Kate, and shook my head, giving a look that said *How could this man possibly be anybody's mentor?* But he was right.

"Have you ever gone on an expedition with a woman?" she asked.

I shot a glance at Max.

"I'd like to go on more expeditions with women," I replied. "Men like Max get boring after too many days and nights."

"I'm curious. How did a boy born in Knoxville, Tennessee, manage to graduate from Princeton and become an international adventurer?"

I laughed. "International adventurer? Please. Who coined that term?"

"I did. And I like it."

"I like adventure journalist."

"How did you get your start in writing?"

"I wrote a series of articles for the Princeton paper when I was the editor, and *National Geographic* picked them up. That started magazine writing for me and helped me land a job on a Chicago paper."

"Ever thought of settling down, having a family?"

"I'm twenty-seven, Kate. Maybe in another decade. Yourself?"

"We're the same age."

"That wasn't my question," I said.

"I know."

Our first course arrived and we began to eat. Kate stopped us.

"Please allow me to say a prayer of thanks," she said, adding, "and a request for safekeeping."

She blessed the food and asked for God's protection on our upcoming trip. As she prayed for her missing brother, I sat there, my eyes open, glancing at Max. He looked amused and took a sip from his small glass.

"Amen," she finally said.

"Amen," the Colonel said in a respectful way.

I nodded and continued eating.

"Not a praying man?" she asked me.

"Only when I have to be."

"Ah, the worst kind."

"What would God possibly care about this meal?" I asked.

"It's called giving thanks. Everything we have—this meal, this roof over our head, the safety in our travels, each breath we breathe—everything is a gift from God."

"I got mugged on the ship," I said. "Was that one of God's angels?"

Kate didn't look provoked. She glanced over at Max and asked a similar question. "What are your thoughts on praying?"

"I talk to God all the time," Max said, reeling her in.

"That's good to hear."

"*Oui*. I ask him time and again where he went, why he left us down here, why he gave up so quickly. Why he made this little mess called the world and then abandoned us. I talk to him, but my dear Kate, he never talks back."

I could see that she wanted to say something, that her eyes and mind all had something to say, but she held back. The Colonel picked up the conversation he'd been having with Max before, breaking the slight moment of tension.

"He still has some issues to work out," I said to Kate.

"At least he knows he does," she replied.

Again, I was stumped. I had been trying to offer a simple bit of encouragement, and somehow felt pricked doing so.

She looked me down with those green-blue eyes that said they wanted to spar. But I knew this was just the first night. We would have plenty of time together; this was supposed to be the honeymoon where everyone was enjoying everyone else.

We spoke about trips we had taken, and I finally began to do what I feel I do best—tell stories and make people laugh. Listening to me were Kate, Max, Colonel Cuaron, the tall Swede Anton Ragnvaludsson, several of the Colonel's men, Dr. Helton (who had also come with Kate and her party), and a couple of waiters. Not everyone understood what I was saying, but they were listening nevertheless.

Just as I was in the middle of a story about the time I was in Spain, Kate stood up. I paused.

"No, keep talking, please," she said, without another word or look of apology.

She walked down to the end of the table where Dr. Helton sat, quiet and stuck between two foreigners who didn't speak English. He was a small man with glasses and big teeth. He was another person I hadn't known was coming—but I welcomed any doctor who was willing to brave the wilderness with us.

As Kate took a chair next to the doctor, I continued my story as if it didn't matter. But suddenly I noticed something. The desire to tell my story well and make everyone laugh had left me.

As I spoke, I watched Kate talking to Dr. Helton. Her eyes and face lit up as she spoke, then listened to the awkward man reply. Even though I was still busy entertaining, I saw something that I admired.

Kate made the doctor feel comfortable.

I finished my story, feeling let down. The punch line is just not the same when your audience suddenly stands up and walks away.

Still, I couldn't fault her. I hadn't even noticed the doctor was at our table. It's hard to notice much else when you're sitting next to someone like Kate.

I swam with dolphins.

It was clear ocean water and I dived under, opening my eyes but not feeling the burn that follows with saltwater. I stayed under for a long time, watching the friendly beasts gliding around me.

"Turn on the light," one dolphin said.

Since when did dolphins talk? Maybe in South America they did. But how did they know English?

"Henry, get up."

I wondered how they knew my name as I sat up and saw a blast of light. I squinted my eyes as I took in my surroundings. It was the hotel room in Rio. I must've been sleeping for at least an hour or two after everyone dispersed from the dinner.

At my doorway stood Max. I knew it wasn't time to get up.

"We have a problem," he said, his face looking a little older than usual.

"What's wrong?"

I sat at the edge of the bed, the fan in the corner doing little to lessen the stifling heat in the room. The slight breeze on my bare back felt good.

"The Colonel's right-hand man—Mateo. We met him tonight before dinner. He was found in an alley a few streets over, his throat slit."

I rubbed my eyes. Max looked serious and tired.

"Who told you?"

"The Colonel himself. One of his men found him."

"Does Kate know?"

Max shook his head. "No. The Colonel said he would tell her in the morning."

"Great way to start a trip."

It took me a few moments to put on my pants and shirt. I followed Max downstairs to the empty and echoing lobby of the grand hotel.

"I apologize for the hour," the Colonel said, looking no different than he had several hours ago.

I wasn't even sure what hour it was.

"No—please. I'm sorry to hear about your man. Do you know what happened?"

"No. One of my men went to Mateo's room and found him missing," Colonel Cuaron said in his thick accent. "This is not like Mateo, especially the night before an expedition. They think he was killed in his room and then taken out."

"Who did it?"

"I told you—the Prescott family has a lot of enemies," Max said.

"But why Mateo?"

If the Colonel had any ideas, he wasn't offering them.

"Maybe to send us a sign," Max said.

"What sign would that be?"

"Go home while you're still alive."

"Don't share that thought with Kate," I told him.

"Mateo was our best guide," the Colonel said. "There are those in this country who don't want foreigners coming into their land to search for anything. Those who prefer to let secrets be secrets. To let the unseen stay unseen."

"Has this ever happened to you before?" I asked.

"Many things happen. I can find another man to fill Mateo's place."

"Did he have a family?"

"No."

"What about any of the other men?" I asked. "Should we check on them?"

"I talked to Anton," Max said. "He's checked on Kate and her party—they're all fine."

"Maybe it has nothing to do with this trip," I said.

"And maybe you just happened to run into me on the way to visiting Hemingway in Key West," Max said.

The Colonel excused himself, leaving us alone.

"I've suddenly got bad feelings about this," I said.

"Suddenly? It takes you long enough, my boy. I had concerns the moment they told me about this trip. That's why I said no."

"Once we get into the wilderness, people will stop following us."

"That will be the least of our concerns once we get into the jungle," Max said. "We should try to get a little more sleep."

"Yeah, okay."

"And Henry? You're sleeping in my room."

I went to object, but Max interrupted me. "I'm not finding you in a back alley tonight. No. If so, they will have to kill both of us."

"Such comforting words."

LEAVING RIO

January 21, 1929

I awoke at sunrise and strolled the streets. The day would be fierce with heat, but this morning was gentle with a breeze that smelled like the ocean. There is nothing better than enjoying the soft glow of a brand-new day. It's like smelling your mother's bread in the oven or the top of a baby's head after its bath. There is something refreshing in the simple pleasure of a breath of wind and the brightening blush of the sky.

I write with fondness, gushing with fondness actually, because of the memory of that morning and everything that followed. We were full of anticipation for the trip, the adventure. Walking down the street past smiling strangers, past happy conversation, past life already in motion, I was almost giddy.

But none of us could have imagined that a place so beautiful, so serene, and so magical could turn into something so terrible.

I wouldn't feel a peace like that again for some time.

I must have pictured striding into the jungle on foot with a small group of men, machete in hand, gun strapped on my side. The reality was nothing like this, and for a second I was a little disappointed when I saw the caravan of cars outside the hotel, all devoted to the Prescott expedition.

There were a couple of Ford cars—a gray Model A and a new-looking blue Model A—along with an older dark Lincoln. I found Max standing on the corner of the street as two of the Colonel's men loaded the vehicles.

"Mr. Prescott wants his son found," Max told me. "This looks to be serious business."

"I somehow never pictured *driving* off into the jungle."

He took the last drag from his cigarette. "There will be miles' worth of jungle that are impossible to walk through, much less drive. Don't worry. These will only take us so far."

I looked around, but didn't see Kate. Anton passed by with a load of supplies.

"Is Miss Prescott ready?"

"She will be coming in a few minutes."

One of the Colonel's men, short and slender with dark skin and friendly eyes, came up to Max and me and pointed.

"You want our bags?" I asked. Obviously the man didn't speak any English.

"I'm guessing we're going with him."

I pointed at the Ford cars and the Lincoln, and he said no. I think that was the only English word he knew.

Another man, stubby-faced and dark-haired, walked by. He didn't look like a local. He stared at me and nodded. He was short and bulky, and looked out of shape by the way he was sweating.

"Who's that?" I asked Max.

"His name is Sonny. I think he's with Kate."

Several minutes passed before Kate appeared. She looked like a movie star, standing there on the corner of the street in her white hat, white shirt, and khaki pants. Normally I would have made a joke, reminding her we were driving off into the wilderness, but I was more curious to see what her frame of mind was this morning.

"Are you okay?" I asked.

Her eyes scanned mine, then looked away, back at the cars. "Are *you* okay, Mr. Wolfe?"

I waited for a moment, waiting to see if she would look at me again. She didn't.

"I doubt you asked any of the men here if they were 'okay.'" This time she looked at me and held her gaze.

I looked toward Max, but he simply glanced at me, waiting just as Kate did for a response.

"I wanted to see how you were—after the news this morning—"

"If you're fumbling for words to find a way to ask if I'm apprehensive after the matter last night, the answer is no."

"Maybe I should have simply said good morning."

"Yes, maybe." She walked off.

The short, dark-haired man, Italian in his features, picked up Kate's suitcase and walked her toward the blue Ford. I looked at Max and shook my head.

"Why is it that women have to be so difficult sometimes?" I asked him.

He chuckled. "Because if they weren't, they would be like you and me. So utterly boring. That's what gives them their allure, their intrigue, their mystery."

"They don't make any sense."

"Le coeur a ses raisons que la raison ne connaît point."

I looked at him. "Thanks. That helps."

"When will you ever learn French?"

"I don't like Frenchmen," I said with a smile.

He sighed. "Pascal. The heart has its reasons which reason knows nothing of."

Before I could reply, there was a loud blast that sounded like a gunshot. Turning the corner was a black and dull yellow Dodge taxi that looked like it could fall apart any second. It rumbled down the street and shook to a halt in front of us.

The small man we had seen earlier popped out of the car, beaming. Our ride had arrived.

It was hard to talk to Max above the sound of the engine dying. That's what it was doing. Dying. It was a long, slow, torturous death, and it wanted us to know its pain. We could feel every bump and hole and rock on the roads. The seat Max and I sat on must have been filled with concrete instead of padding. My buttocks felt numb and I had to move my legs to keep them from falling asleep.

But, amidst all of this, not to mention the heat that felt like two swollen, searing gloves clamped around my neck, the driver, Paulo, sang songs in Portuguese that made it sound like we were having the best day of our lives.

The plan was to be on the road most of the day, heading to the village of Carasack. The road part would be the shortest leg of the journey, and judging by my body, maybe the most uncomfortable.

"Who is that Italian with Kate?" I hollered to Max.

"Not sure."

"Doesn't look like the friendliest."

"We didn't come here to make friends."

I pointed at the driver. "I think Paulo did. He seems quite happy."

"Happiness is all about perspective, wouldn't you agree?"

I thought about walking over the bridge on a cold wintry night in Chicago, the four men behind me waiting to kill me.

I nodded my agreement. Happiness is all about perspective. Yes, I felt suffocated with heat, and my ears were weary from the noise. I couldn't feel much below my belt, and the road seemed endless and unexciting.

But I was alive, breathing in the exotic air of another country. Yes, happiness is about perspective.

The bad diesel smell wafting over us—the kind of odor one might smell before an engine explodes—I decided I would just ignore that and concentrate on Paulo's uplifting songs.

If only I could know of the adventures he sang about.

The sun was starting to slip away when we reached the bridge over the large river. Two men guarded it. By the time our car caught up with the three in front, we could see that something was wrong.

We pulled up, and the engine belched to a stop. Max and I welcomed any chance to get out. We stood by the side of our car and took in the scene.

The bridge looked old, but sturdy enough for our vehicles. There were two men with rifles, and a third sitting on a stone wall at the side of the road watching. The two guards were talking with the Colonel. Other than the appearance of the rifles, this didn't seem out of the ordinary.

Max offered me some water, and I was about to take it when the situation by the bridge suddenly changed. I could hear yelling in a foreign language. One of the guards pointed at the cars, then at the bridge. The Colonel was talking but it looked like they weren't paying attention. Suddenly, one of the riflemen rushed to the parked cars and jerked open the door. He reached in and pulled out the figure in white.

The figure was Kate.

The man grabbed her by the arm as she came along, saying nothing. He pulled her toward the bridge, shouting something at the other guards. The rest of the men from the cars poured out, and suddenly everything was very tense, very dangerous.

The man holding Kate pointed a rifle at the rest of our group. The other rifleman was also belting out commands.

The Italian, Sonny, walked closer to the men. The Colonel looked at him and put up a hand.

"It's okay, things are fine," he said, his palm facing toward us, waving at everyone, letting us know it was okay.

But the men at the bridge were still shouting, and Kate looked pale in the afternoon sun.

The Colonel was talking, putting up both hands, the men shouting, the rifles pointed at us.

And then, in a blur and a flash, it all changed.

Sonny made a move. I heard one shot, another, a third, and then I looked up to see Kate shriek and move to one side as the rifleman next to her slumped down on the ground, his rifle dropping. The other rifleman dropped his gun and clutched his stomach, looking terror-stricken. A fourth shot was fired and hit him below the neck, leveling him.

The third man, the one by the bridge, jumped to his feet, but only to raise his arms in surrender.

Sonny rushed toward Kate, his pistol still aimed at the riflemen.

"No, no, no," the Colonel said.

There was a rush of activity and noise and voices as everybody tried to take in what had just happened. Sonny put an arm around Kate, who was distraught and in tears.

"Let's keep going," I heard him say to the Colonel as they climbed back into the car.

Even our friendly driver looked confused and frightened. Max, seemingly unfazed at everything, slowly climbed back into our car.

"Now we know why the Italian came along," he said.

THE TOWN OF DESEMBOQUE

January 24, 1929

We had landed in the middle of a revolution.

I'm still not sure who was fighting whom or for what, but the second town we stopped in on our way to the Paracatu River appeared to be in the midst of a civil war. We had been in the city just a couple hours when men in strange military garb carrying old rifles and guns marched past as if they were playing war and not going to it. That was the first sign that we were stuck in Desemboque, a small thumbprint of a town in the Brazilian countryside tucked beside the mountains and jungle to the north and west.

On our third day, I found myself bored and wondering why I had accepted this trip. So far there had been little adventure. Our car had broken down four times; each time Paulo got out and sang and somehow fixed it. Another one of the cars had tire problems, but he fixed that too. I'd seen or spoken to Kate very little, and I thought the daughter of the man responsible for this expedition selfish and rude. The last two nights, stuck in this village trying to have some sort of fun, Max and I had found ourselves in a local tavern by ourselves, no sign of Kate anywhere.

It was the third evening in Desemboque and I walked a dirt road, passing a small store that sold random items from gum to rifles and everything in between. Only yesterday I had found a brown Borsalino outback hat, a slightly more comfortable fedora that fit me better than the hat I was wearing. I also bought a vintage .45 handgun, a M1911 that seemed to still have a long life ahead of it. It came with a holster, a combination I'd never had but decided would be good in case an animal decided to lunge at me or I got caught up in the middle of a Brazilian battle.

I was passing a small sidewalk café and noticed the blondish brown locks first. Kate, sipping a coffee. I couldn't see anyone else.

"I thought you had packed up and gone home."

"How are you, Mr. Wolfe?"

"It's Henry. I'm bored. But doing well. Like my new hat?"

"It's a little rough around the edges. Suits you."

"May I sit?" I asked.

"Certainly."

I sat across from her and looked around. The town gave me a strange sensation of having been left behind. Many of the local men had been summoned to join the revolution. Locals had asked us to stay put until they came back. I wasn't sure where exactly they had gone—to war? To protest? To have a party? All I knew is that we were foreigners and were asked to stay here for now.

"Feeling anxious?" I asked.

"Do you have siblings, Mr. Wolfe?"

"The *Mr. Wolfe* is getting tiresome."

"Do you?"

"A younger brother and sister."

"Then imagine your beloved sister somewhere out there, in this faraway place, lost or trapped or even something worse."

I nodded.

"To you," she continued, "this is an adventure, an anecdote to use at a party, a tale to tell in another book. But for me, for my family, this is our life. Louis may be dead, but we're hoping and praying that he is alive, and that we find him. So yes, Mr. Wolfe—*Henry*—I am feeling anxious, and will probably continue to feel anxious until I learn the truth."

I tightened my lips and nodded. Thankfully a waitress came out then and asked what I wanted to drink.

I said, *"Cerveja,"* which meant beer. One of the few Portuguese words I knew.

For a few minutes we sat there, a slight breeze blowing on us. I didn't mind the silence. I was grateful for company other than Max.

"I'm sorry," Kate said.

"For what?"

"For snapping at you."

"It's fine. I understand. I shouldn't be so nonchalant about finding your brother."

"I know the general sentiment. I know that it's unlikely that we will find him. But I also believe in the power of prayer."

"I'm not sure how much that's going to help us, but every little thing counts."

"When I was a young girl, Louis was involved in a shooting accident. He lost a lot of blood, and we thought we were going to lose him. For two straight days our family prayed over him. The doctors didn't give him long to live. But those prayers were answered. God allowed Louis to live."

"I'm sure the doctors helped out too."

"You're a skeptic, are you not?"

I took a sip of the lukewarm beer. "I'm a realist. I have nothing against praying. You can pray to a donkey if you want to. I just have never known any of that to work for me."

"It's not about having it 'work for you.' "

"Yeah, well, to each his own then."

"What do you think we'll find in the jungle?"

"I'm just waiting to get into the jungle."

For a moment Kate stared at me. Then she produced some letters from her handbag. They looked like they had been unfolded and refolded many times.

"These were the final few letters we received from Louis. The last came a month after he disappeared." She handed them to me.

I opened the first and noticed the small, deliberate handwriting.

To my beloved family:

I am about to embark on a grand adventure. This place is unlike anywhere I've been. It's bigger than my dreams allowed it to be. I enter the expedition with many expectations and nervous anticipations. I do not know if I will find Fawcett or even answers to his disappearance, but I hope I will find something. A place like this is ripe for stories. I hope this quest will prove to be one worth telling.

I pray for safety and for guidance. I know God will protect me.

I love you and look forward to seeing your faces soon.

Louis

I glanced at Kate.

"He's a romantic, isn't he?" she said without looking at me. "He's a fan of yours, by the way."

"Don't hold that against him."

"Read the next one. It took a long time getting to us, but it eventually found its way to civilization."

For my family:

My trip has taken an unexpected turn. The trail to Fawcett has proved fruitless, but in my travels I've discovered something else. Two different tribes have spoken about "everlasting life." It seems they believe that deep in the heart of this country lies a place where the sick can be healed and the living cannot die.

I have uncovered a map to this place, with certain clues, certain villages and rivers that are known and many others that are not. I myself am not positive where I am. The Indians are guiding me. I'm thankful to have materials to barter with.

I send this rudimentary map to give you an idea. In case anything happens to us, I want you to know where I am.

Louis

"What happened to the map?" I asked.

"Anton has it. No one else, apart from my family, knows about it."

"It seems like everybody else has a map but me," I said, thinking of the one Max had. "So why tell me?"

Kate brushed back her hair and took a slight breath. She glanced at the letters in my hand, then back out at the street. There was no one else in sight.

"I don't know you, Henry, but I did read your book. And the strange thing is—I don't know why, but more than anyone else on this expedition, apart from Sonny of course, the only person I feel I can trust is you."

"I appreciate you saying that, but I'm not sure I understand why."

"Did you really go back for Kalila?"

I nodded. "The story really happened. Everything in that book is true."

"It's just—it's hard to believe. And despite—I don't agree with your outlook on life or with certain attitudes or actions—but any man who would go back . . . It was an honorable thing to do."

I finished my beer. "And I was getting the impression you hated me."

Kate smiled. It was a sad smile. "Saying that you did an honorable thing is not saying I love you."

"Forgive me," I said. "Didn't mean to get ahead of myself."

"I don't know if the map will help us, just as I don't know if my brother is alive or dead. It was his fault for being so stupid, coming here in the first place, thinking that he could do something as brazen and foolish as going into the wilderness with little experience. I just know that—well, read the final letter."

This one looked like it had water damage, and I couldn't read all of it. Some of the ink had bled over, and another chunk appeared to be missing.

"I'm surprised we even got that much," Kate said.

To my family:

The great city exists, and there are many who

The writing was smudged, and I couldn't finish the sentence.

dangerous and treacherous. Don't trust anyone. But it's real.

I'm uncertain what I will find. But I know it's here. I've seen it with my own two eyes.

I hope God hears my prayers. Because this place is only filled with devils.

That was all that was left—the rest of the letter was torn away beneath this ominous beginning.

"This is the last you heard from him?"

"Yes. And it doesn't quite end on an optimistic note."

"He found something."

"Yes, but what? And if they didn't want it found—if nobody has come across this so-called lost city in the jungle for so many years—how can it be found now?"

"Why did you come, Kate?"

She looked at me, her defenses suddenly up again, those eyes ready to fight. "What's that mean?"

"It means, why did you come? You could have sent a dozen expeditions and not come yourself."

"Are you saying that I can't—"

"I'm saying that you didn't have to come down here to worry your family. You didn't *need* to come on this expedition. People like Max and me—we're the type to go on trips like this. It's not a male-female thing I'm talking about. The Colonel and Anton and all of the men—they're all very capable."

"But I don't trust them. Sonny I trust. And—well, in many ways I trust you too."

"Why is trust such a big thing?"

"Because there are secrets and mysteries out there that people don't want discovered. And along with that, there are rumors of treasures, and that always brings out the worst in men. And I believe—I know—I feel God wanted me on this expedition."

"So it comes down to your faith."

Kate looked away for a moment. "I know how that must sound to a man like you."

I shrugged. "I'm not a cannibal, Kate. I respect your faith. And your love for your brother. How can I have anything to say against that?"

"I know it might seem naïve."

"Yes, it does. But it also seems real. I don't understand it. And if your God really wanted you to come along on this expedition, I'm not sure what that says about him. Seems like a dangerous thing to send anyone to."

"Then why did you come?"

I smiled at her. "Look at this place. Some village most people in the world have never heard of. They know about New York and Chicago and even Rio. But Desemboque? Uh-uh. These are the moments I relish. Sitting in a faraway place knowing that the rest of the world doesn't know about it. And you know what else?"

Kate's eyes lit up. "What?"

"To be able to uncover something that nobody else has seen, that there have only been rumors about. That is the thing that makes me wake up in the morning. It doesn't happen often. To think that something could happen to old Max and me again, just like it did in Egypt— well, I have my doubts we'll get lucky twice. But that's why I came."

"Do you still feel as excited as you were when you first heard about it?"

The wind blew her hair. The long strands brushed against her cheek, and I watched her slender hand gently move them back. She was beautiful and enthralling, and seeing her looking at me, not in a combative way, but in an open and friendly way, made my mind whirl.

"I'm very glad to be here," was all I could say.

Max was nowhere to be found.

I hadn't seen him for at least twenty-four hours. Normally I wouldn't be worried, but we were stuck in the middle of an unfamiliar foreign town with lots of people around carrying guns. He'd had ample time to get himself in trouble. I only hoped that the trouble wouldn't be the same as it was for the Colonel's man found dead in the alley the night before we left Rio.

Sweat and rain covered my forehead and cheeks as I walked into the restaurant where most of our group were gathered. Kate was there with Anton, Dr. Helton, and Sonny.

"Any sign of Max?"

They shook their heads collectively.

"The last time I saw him, he had his arm around a woman," Sonny Bettino said.

So far, the only thing I knew about the Italian was that he was short, stocky, and could shoot someone dead with one shot. I had just recently learned his last name. He had a thick cover of several days' worth of beard on his face. He looked hotter than I felt.

I glanced quickly at Kate. "Mind if I sit?"

Anton shook his head and stood up, giving me his seat while he took one next to him in the corner of the table.

"Have you seen the Colonel?"

The Swede nodded. "Gathering supplies. And additional men. We will be at the river soon."

A waitress came by, but I didn't order anything. I needed to go find Max.

"He'll be fine," Sonny said.

"You don't know Max."

"Nothing's going to happen in this town. Nobody's around to make it happen. All the men took off."

"Anything can happen," Anton said.

"Have a beer," Sonny said to me.

I obliged him but didn't care much for the lukewarm beer.

Sonny was talkative tonight. I didn't know if it was the beer or the time on our hands or the fact that we weren't in expedition mode. He laughed at his own jokes, interrupted himself in midsentence, and treated Kate like an old friend.

"You seem to know Kate well," I said to him.

"My family has known Kate's family for—for what? A long time. Ever since my family got off the boat from Italy, right? Something like that."

"It's been awhile," Kate said, subdued. She looked worried.

Sonny continued to talk about his Italian heritage and his family in New York and how he was lucky to be on this trip. Suddenly the door to the restaurant opened. We could hear the rain outside, and then a familiar laugh sounded.

"My dear friends! The revolution is over!"

Max walked in, arm clasped around a woman who stood several inches taller than he. Her wild, curly hair looked extra full from the rain and humidity. She was striking in her beauty but looked dangerous, especially for someone like Max who didn't understand the term *discretion*.

Max walked over and patted me on the back. "It's time to toast to freedom!"

"What are you talking about?" Kate asked.

"The men are back. It's fiesta time. Or siesta. Or whatever they do when they party. *Carnivale*? I don't know."

"Looks like you've been having a fiesta yourself, Mr. Joubert," Sonny said.

I was impressed by his correct pronunciation of Max's last name.

Max ordered some sort of drink that must have been local. They served it in small glasses.

"Try this. It's wonderful."

I looked at the glass. Outside I could hear music and drums playing.

"They're celebrating? Now?"

"The war is over," Max said with a grin.

"Did the war ever begin?" Kate asked.

"I don't think so. Which deserves a celebration, does it not?"

"Excuse me," Kate said, having apparently seen enough.

I wanted to follow her, but I figured she wouldn't want to talk with me. Yesterday was probably ample communication for some time.

I looked at the strange concoction in my hand.

"Go ahead, boy. Drink up. That might be the last drink you have. For some time."

A hundred-and-eighty-five-pound Frenchman is a hard thing to carry.

I wasn't literally carrying him. Not yet. But he had stopped singing and stopped looking in front of him, and if we didn't make it to his bed quickly he would soon stop everything.

Max leaned against me and stepped on my feet and started to collapse, then regained his balance but kept drifting from side to side.

"No more *aguardiente* for you," I told Max.

"She was beautiful, wasn't she? So beautiful."

I laughed. "I don't know, Max. That woman was a little too much for you."

"Fool."

He stumbled, and I helped him back up. "You're not making this easy for me."

"Such a fool."

"I'm not the idiot who can't walk."

"I wasn't talking about that lady back there. Always slow, aren't you?"

"Trying to keep up with you," I said.

"Kalila. She was beautiful, wasn't she?"

I nodded. "One of a kind."

"I will always love her," he said in a strange intoxicated French accent that somehow seemed to fit.

"I know."

"She will always, forever, for all time . . ." He trailed off.

We had reached the door to his room. "Let's just get you to bed."

"I'm not an old man, you know?"

"No, you're a drunk. That's worse."

Max laughed. "No respect for the elderly. None."

"You're lucky I'm not carrying you."

"I've been carrying you your whole career."

That was a little too harsh for my liking. I didn't reply. I helped him to his bed.

"Once a boy, always a boy," he said to me.

"You can be a mean drunk," I said.

"I'm honest. There's a difference."

"Not always."

Max rolled to one side, and I wondered if he was out. I looked around the small hotel room. I doubted Max had slept any in this room. There was a small dresser with a hat resting on top of it. For a second I looked back at Max, his body unmoving. I had just seen him put the hat he was wearing onto the chair. This must be a new one.

It didn't look like a hat Max would buy.

I picked it up by its top and turned it around to see the label, and that's when I heard the furious clicking sound. The dresser moved, turned into something—my eyes weren't connecting or my mind working. Then I saw the white and sandy brown color of reptile skin and the wound coils and the head flailing.

It was the meanest snake I'd ever seen.

And it looked really furious that I'd disturbed its cozy sleep beneath the hat.

I stood there, paralyzed, for what felt like an eternity but was actually only a matter of seconds, and then I saw the swooping glint of a blade crash down next to me and cut off the rattlesnake's head.

Max stood beside me, looking at the part of the snake that now lay on the floor by the door. In his hand was a short machete.

"You don't want to be bit by one of those," Max said, putting the instrument back on the table next to the bed.

"Where'd you get that?"

"It's called a cascavel," he said, ignoring my question. "They're a tad nasty when provoked."

He still looked groggy and, well, drunk.

"I don't know if you should be handling machetes at this time of night."

"And I don't know if you should examine really hideous-looking hats that you know I would never in a million years ever wear."

"How did you—"

"I knew what that was the second I heard the first shake of its very loud rattle."

I sat in the chair, looking at the head of the snake that might have killed me. My heart hadn't had time to catch up with my brain—it was only now beating furiously. I breathed in and out.

"Old man, huh?" Max mumbled.

"I owe you."

"Add it to the list."

He either was oblivious to the facts or too tired to delve into them. But someone had tried to kill him. And had almost succeeded in killing me.

"Wonder what's waiting in your room?" Max said with a chuckle.

"Maybe I'll just—"

"Fine with me. Just make sure you dispose of the snake. These Brazilian monsters sometimes can come back to life."

I gasped, then saw Max turn his head to see if he got me.

When he saw my face, he laughed, knowing he had.

The rain had disappeared and the festive partying had stopped and the village had resumed life as normal. It was already baking outside and it wasn't even eight o'clock yet. I walked outside and put on my hat to shield my eyes from the sun. Quickly approaching steps sounded behind me, and I turned to see Kate, in another hat I hadn't seen, a sharp fashionable khaki skirt, and vest.

"Good morning, Henry."

"Yes, good morning." I was tired, and my mouth wasn't cooperating with my brain.

"You look a bit ragged today."

"Yeah, I feel it too. The coffee didn't even help."

"Trouble sleeping?"

I was about to tell her what had happened when I was interrupted.

"He misses the comforts of home," Max said, coming up behind me and slapping me on the back. I never could understand how he could wake up from a night like the one before looking as refreshed and ready to go as he looked now. "He is longing for the chill of Chicago, aren't you?"

I looked at him and smiled.

"We are finally off," Kate said, a gleam in her eyes.

I thought of the snake and wished I could be as excited.

Kate didn't need to know about it. But I would be keeping my eyes open for her.

And, I hoped, doing a better job of keeping my eyes open for myself.

ON THE PARACATU RIVER

January 28, 1929

It wasn't the noise of the jungle surrounding us that made me nervous. It was the lack of noise. Some days as we paddled down the Paracatu in our four dugout canoes, the first piloted by Anton and Dr. Helton, it seemed as though every life form around us was holding its breath in anticipation of something—the way a room gets quiet right before everyone shouts "Surprise!" for a birthday. It wasn't just that the animals around us knew we were coming. It was as if they knew we didn't belong.

That's why the sound of the howl made Kate jump.

I watched her in the dugout in front of us, headed up by the Colonel himself. Sonny sat in front of her, with Istu, Mateo's replacement, guiding the boat from the back. Our little convoy glided down the slow-moving river: two *camaradas* paddled in Anton's canoe, two more with Max, Paulo, and me, and four brought up the rear in a dugout carrying our supplies.

The camaradas were men the Colonel had enlisted to help take us down the rarely navigated river of the Paracatu that wound its way into the mountainous terrain of the Matto Grosso. They looked like Brazilian pirates, with ragtag shirts and pants and little else. A few of them were black men, a few Latinos, a couple looked European. Most of them worked hard, but as Max had warned me, they were not to be trusted.

Some days our progress was minimal. We needed to be careful about rapids, hidden branches or rocks in the river, blockages that would require getting out of the river and hauling our boats around whatever prevented us from moving ahead.

When the sound came, it was late afternoon. We had already started to look for a good *praia*, or sandbank, to camp on overnight. I could see the glow of Kate's hair as she, remarkably, still had the energy to row. The woman was tough, this I knew. And she made tough look absolutely beautiful.

We had heard a few low grunts coming from the jungle, but this was different. This was a long and booming roar that made me shudder. Kate turned her head one way, then the other.

"What was that?" I asked Max, who was seated behind me.

"A howler monkey," he said, bored. "They sound scary, but really don't do much. Except eat and sleep."

Kate looked back at me. I smiled and waved, wanting her to know that everything was okay. Her forced smile made me feel silly and juvenile.

"Why don't you just share a boat with her?" Max said.

"Just making sure she's not worried."

"I hope the Colonel and the blond know where they're going. My *derriere* can't take much more of this."

I turned around and noticed him resting on his back with his dark face looking up at the sky. Branches that might have been a hundred years old towered over us, the sun and the water irresistible to them at the river's edge.

"It's almost time to stop for the day."

"Thank heavens."

The howler monkey seemed to have found friends, and they sang in a thunderous choir.

"Too bad all the animals aren't as laid-back as our wailing friends."

I looked at Max. "What's that mean?"

He laughed. "We're on foreign soil. That's why the animals out there are quiet, for the most part. Because we're invading their territory."

"They're animals, not the French."

"Let's just hope none of them get testy."

The fire had been lit for at least an hour, with our group tucked around it finishing dinner and telling stories. The camaradas kept to themselves, not because we wanted them to, but because they preferred it. The usual routine was that Paulo, the singing happy member of the Colonel's group, tried to make fire. Istu would argue with him in a language I didn't understand and then make the fire himself.

Anton ate more and said less than anyone else. Sometimes I wasn't sure if he understood what we were saying, or if he cared. Max would joke and tell stories, and depending on my energy level, I would do the same. Kate was usually combative, finding someone to disagree with. Sonny chimed in every now and then or went to sleep early.

On this evening we were talking about the howler monkey we'd heard earlier in the day.

"I got the impression that there were going to be man-eating alligators everywhere," Kate said.

"I've seen a few today," Max said.

"They don't like strangers," the Colonel said in his mild voice. "They sink into the water when our boats come."

Kate looked enamored. "Everyone told me to be careful about them."

"I once almost stepped on the head of a fifteen-foot black caiman," Anton said. "I thought it was a stone. I was a very lucky man."

I thought of telling the snake story to add some flair to the conversation, but then realized that the snake didn't just randomly happen to be in the hotel room.

"So what animal do you fear the most?" Kate asked the Colonel in her typical bold fashion.

With no thought or hesitancy he replied, "The piranha."

The Colonel's quick response made the entire group pause. It wasn't a good pause either, but the kind that happens when you arrive at a fork in the road or when you're peering off the edge of a cliff.

"Are they that bad?" Kate finally asked.

"Only if they are stirred up," the Colonel said. "They hunt in groups, attacking prey their own size or smaller. They are always in groups of a hundred. I've seen them attack animals and even humans, however."

"Why?"

Max chimed in. "Those foul little creatures are straight out of a nightmare. Have you ever seen them up close? They're as mean and furious as they look. The teeth—the jaws—that want to bite something. They're savage little monsters."

"They are drawn to blood," Colonel Cuaron continued. "So if an animal is bleeding, it can be dangerous."

"Dangerous as in how?" Kate asked.

"I'm thinking of chicken bones myself," Max said.

"They are very dangerous," the Colonel said, leaving it at that.

After several minutes of this conversation, Anton, who had been dozing off by the campfire, sat up and looked around.

"Where is the doctor?" he asked.

We all looked at Anton, then looked around. Usually the doctor retired early for the evening in one of the tents that had been set up around the praia.

"Isn't he in his tent?" Kate asked.

For a man who had just been resting with his eyes closed, Anton had the energy of an attacking lion. He jumped up and checked several tents.

"He told me he was going off with Istu in search of something to eat," Sonny said.

"That was, what, an hour ago?" I asked him.

"I assumed—I don't know."

"Colonel, is Istu back?"

There was commotion for a moment, as we checked tents, asked the rest of the men, looked around the perimeter of the camp, called out names. The doctor and Istu were nowhere to be found.

"We need to find them," Anton said, grabbing a rifle. "Max. Henry. Come with me."

After talking about flesh-eating animals and the dangers of the wilderness, I wasn't sure how happy I was to be going off into the dark night looking for the two men. But I couldn't say no. Kate looked at me, and I needed to be as courageous as the others. She didn't need to know I was terrified.

You can go ahead," Max said once we were beyond sight of the camp and its orange glow.

"Such a gentleman," I said, my face swatting into a branch. "So considerate, too."

As opposed to earlier in the day when the jungle seemed to be muffled, the sound of life around us was overwhelming. Everything vibrated.

I could hear Anton several steps in front of me. I kept running into something. A tree, a rock, a monkey—I wasn't sure. I couldn't make out much in the dense brush.

"Doctor? Istu?" Anton called out.

"Do you know where we're going?" I asked him.

"Just stay by me," the Swede said.

"Keep talking then. I can't see a thing."

For a moment we kept walking, with Anton calling out their names. I stopped after a while and turned around, not hearing anything behind me.

"Max?"

There was nothing. Nothing but silence.

Anton continued to call out their names, moving ahead in the dark jungle.

"Max? You there, Max?"

Something grabbed my arm and made me jump.

"Right here, dear boy," he said. "It's dark out here, huh?"

"You still have your rifle?" I asked him.

"Sure. But if something comes out of the dark to get us, I might end up shooting you."

"It's so refreshing having you around."

But hearing Max's laugh was refreshing. It almost made it seem like we were back home, back on a university campus joking about life. Almost made you forget that you were hiking through an uncharted jungle looking for a missing doctor.

Almost.

Did you hear that?"

Max stopped and held out his hand. For a few minutes we just stood there in the middle of the jungle trying to be silent and still.

I waited for him to keep walking. A minute later, the sound came again.

"Max," I whispered.

I could see the outline of his hand bidding me to stop.

We both knew the sound.

It was somewhere between a cough and a growl. Not overly

intimidating in itself. But terrifying when you realized what it belonged to.

"They don't attack, do they?" I asked him.

"When men don't shut their mouths, they do."

We waited for ten, maybe fifteen minutes.

"Max?"

"Yes."

"How long are we going to wait?"

"That was a jaguar."

"I know that. What should we do?"

"My sense is that it was close by."

"Your sense?" I asked in a frantic whisper. "That thing was smelling my armpit."

"If that's the case, he would be far away right around now."

As if to answer Max's comment, a high-pitched scream tore through the mostly quiet jungle. My blood froze, and I turned all around, trying to see where the noise was coming from.

"Anton!" I called out.

"Shut your mouth," Max ordered.

"Who was that?"

The screaming went on for another minute. High-pitched wailing, such as I'd never heard before. Wild, brash, violent screaming.

And then, just as suddenly, it stopped.

As though the record had been smashed in two.

"Who was that?" I asked again.

"It wasn't Anton."

"How do you know?"

"It was the doctor," Max said.

"Do you think—?"

"Yes."

We stood there, waiting. I could feel my forehead and cheeks lined with sweat, the rest of my body coated as well.

"Have you ever seen the forepaws on a jaguar?" Max asked.

"Why don't you describe them to me?" I said, adrenaline-laced sarcasm racing through me.

"They have long claws that help pin down and hold their prey. Their tongues are designed for peeling the skin of their victim away."

"That's great to know, professor."

"Why don't you go ahead and check on Anton?"

"What?"

"Lower your voice," Max said, sitting down to rest against a tree.

"Why don't *you* go and check on Anton?"

"You're younger. You can run faster."

I laughed. "You're smarter. You'll know where to run."

Max got back up. We were both too nervous to do anything except not act nervous.

"If you get mauled, he'll have a better meal with you. I'm all skin and bones."

"Old bones, too," I said.

"They're known to climb trees," Max said.

"Shut up."

"They'll watch their prey from above, then jump on them when they're not expecting it."

"I've got a gun," I said.

"You're too slow."

"This isn't funny."

"I'm not trying to be."

"What are we going to do?"

"First, dear boy, we need to—"

A figure darted out of the woods, then a shot went off. Then I heard running and a shriek and I couldn't tell which of those things I had caused.

"Put the gun down!" a voice said.

I dropped my gun. "I didn't mean to—it didn't—"

"Not you. Fool!"

I heard Anton taking Max's gun.

"Good thing it was pointed down," Max said to the Swede. "I almost shot you."

"What happened?" I asked, realizing I had fired off a shot into the darkness.

"Next time why don't you two make a little more noise?" Anton said. "The doctor. He's dead."

Max cursed while I stood there, frozen again.

"Come on. I need you both to help me with his body."

"Why?" I asked.

"Each of us can carry a part," Anton said, already walking back into the jungle.

The fire crackled and sent ashes floating high into the dark night above the campground. I watched it in a stupor, hypnotized by the glow and the heat. I didn't want to think about what had just happened, how that could have easily been Max or Kate or me or anybody else, what it would be like being out here without a doctor, and especially how I could face Kate tomorrow.

But as a sound nudged me out of my half coma, I knew that I wouldn't have to wait that long.

"Hi," she said quietly.

I started to stand, but she waved for me not to.

"Mind if I sit?" she asked.

"No. Please."

She sat next to me, surprisingly close. She shivered, and I knew it wasn't because of the temperature.

"How are you doing?"

She started to reply, then shook her head. She suddenly put her face into her hands and began to sob. I put an arm around her and let her cry against me.

"It's okay," I said.

She shook, and I held her more tightly. I looked around to see if there was anybody else up, but nobody could be seen.

Kate shook her head and wiped her eyes. "I'm sorry. Really, I'm sorry. It's just—I'm just—it's just—"

"No, I know. A thing."

She cleared her voice. "A 'thing'?"

"Yeah. A woman thing. I know—I have a sister."

I didn't expect the laugh coming from her. "A 'woman thing'?"

"It's fine—I understand. Sometimes you just can't help it."

"You idiot."

"Excuse me?" I asked.

Again she laughed. "It's not a 'woman thing,' Henry."

"Then—"

"One of our men—one of *my* men—just got ripped apart in the woods. I have every right to cry over him and not have it be considered a 'woman thing.'"

"Yeah, of course—I'm . . ."

She hadn't needed to call me an idiot. I fully realized I was one.

For a long time we sat there in silence.

"Look, it's just . . ." Kate paused, then continued. "It's a terrified-of-things-that-crawl-in-the-jungle-at-night *thing*."

I nodded. "Yeah, okay."

She started to cry again, or laugh, or do both. I was confused, tired, and had just helped cart off part of a body.

I might be losing my mind.

"Henry?"

"Yes."

"Can I ask you a favor?"

"Sure."

She breathed in, thinking for a minute. "Would you mind—I don't mean to be inappropriate, but would you mind maybe sleeping outside my tent?"

For a moment I'd thought I had heard her say *inside*, and my head really started to drift. But I knew that wasn't the case.

"Sure, of course."

"It's just—well, Sonny, as you know, snores. And I just—"

"No, it's fine, please."

She looked up at me with childlike eyes, the kind that look gentle and sweet, the kind that look generous and thankful.

"Want to talk about it?" I asked.

"No."

I nodded. For a minute we just looked into the fire. So far away from civilization, it was nice to have her there, by my side.

I chanced to look at her, a strong profile, with deep soft eyes that pondered who knows what.

Then she stood up and touched my shoulder. "Thanks."

I wanted to say something witty or profound or meaningful, but nothing came out. I just nodded and waited for her to crawl back into her tent. Then I stretched out in front of it, feeling woefully insufficient as a bodyguard, but glad she'd asked me anyway.

STILL ON THE PARACATU RIVER

January 30, 1929

It rained for two days after the doctor's death. It seemed appropriate. Both Max and I tried our best to take the focus off the obvious, to add a little levity to the situation, but nobody wanted anything to do with it. It wasn't just a death in the wilderness that was the problem. It was the manner of death. A jaguar attacking a human was almost unheard of, and it had several camaradas among our group worried.

The Colonel was worried too.

It was dusk, and thankfully Istu had found us a jacu, a turkey-like bird that actually wasn't too bad. I was glad that the rain had momentarily stopped, that there was a fire to get dry by, and that I didn't have to go off into the jungle to hunt. Or to find a missing member of our group.

That's when Colonel Cuaron asked me to take a walk. It wasn't the sort of question you said no to.

"I have spoken with Mr. Joubert about this," he began as we walked along the river, out of earshot of the rest of the camp.

"What's wrong?"

The Colonel kept walking until we reached a small opening underneath massive trees. It was good to stand after sitting in the dugouts for so many hours. We looked out over the river. The clear water was steady and soft; I could have lain on the sand and slept for ten hours.

"The camaradas are worried, and it's not just because of the doctor's death."

I nodded, waiting to hear what he would say.

"The Paracatu River flows into another river, the Tuiche. The Prescott party went down the Tuiche. Many say that it is cursed."

"Do you believe that?" I asked.

"Many Indians in these parts do, and so do some of the men. The incident with the doctor confirmed these fears."

"But what do you think?"

His congenial face looked strained and serious. "I believe that jaguars don't attack humans unless absolutely necessary. The viciousness of the attack—I believe that was unusual."

"So what do we do?"

The Colonel looked at me with a gaze that didn't let go. "Kate trusts you. She is worried, as she probably should be. I know that she has her Italian friend who is fond of using guns, but you need to watch her. Keep your eyes on her all the time."

"No problem," I said. "Why is the river supposedly cursed?"

"It doesn't matter. And I don't know if such things are real. I've never gone down the Tuiche myself. I just know that some of the Indians around the river have been known to be unfriendly."

"Unfriendly, meaning . . . ?"

"Unfriendly," the Colonel said. "I just want you to see that Kate is protected. I've asked Max to make sure the men don't abandon us." He turned as if to head toward our camp.

"Colonel?"

He looked back at me.

"Do you think there's any chance that we'll find Louis Prescott?"

He shook his head, looking downriver at the fading light. Everything was remarkably still.

"I don't want Mr. Prescott to lose a daughter as well as a son. She shouldn't be out here."

I understood.

Maybe there was a curse on this river or the next. Maybe the jaguar attack was unusual and should have sent us packing. Maybe there were unfriendly Indians watching us at that very moment. I didn't care about any of that. All I cared about were the nasty little flying demons that were everywhere. After the rains died down, the insects flared up. They were the real curse. We couldn't do anything —eat, sleep, breathe—without having a face full of mosquitoes or gnats.

As we sat around the fire, Max kept swinging his hand around his face, swearing up a storm. The more he waved his arm, the more the insects swarmed around his head.

He sneezed and looked at me, eyes watery and bugs all around him.

"They must like Frenchmen," I said, with a chuckle.

None of us was laughing the next morning. Termites had gotten into Anton's belongings and eaten half of his duffel bag, part of his hat, and most of his long underwear. We saw him holding the underwear by the fire the next morning and burning it.

I was covered in insect bites, some of them red and swollen.

Kate said little. Her beautifully flawless skin was blemished like the rest of us; the insects seemed to like her even more than Max. But she never complained.

As we started out on this morning, I asked her if I could go in her dugout.

"I'm quite all right on my own."

"I just think it best to be careful."

"That's why Sonny is here."

I didn't want to point out the other night.

"Maybe this is my excuse to be in your company all day."

The eyes lit up, and her smile couldn't help making the rest of her face shine. "Why didn't you say that in the first place? I'd love to have you join me."

The Colonel agreed to switch places with me.

Which, as it turned it out, may have saved my life.

This river is utterly confusing," Kate said, taking a break from paddling as our heavy canoe continued steadily behind Anton in the lead dugout.

Sonny was in the front of the boat, Kate behind him and me next. Istu was at the rear, paddling mechanically as though he never tired.

"Too many twists and turns?" I asked.

"It's like a snake that's constantly on the move."

"Male or female?" I asked, playing with her.

"Excuse me?"

"Well, if it's like a snake, is it male or female?"

"Definitely female," she said, looking out at the trees along the river and catching my eye in her peripheral view.

"And why is that?"

"It's way too exotic and striking to be a male."

"So what are you saying about men?"

She turned, her eyebrows raised. "I can say a lot."

Sonny heard this and laughed.

"Stai zitto!" Kate said.

He chuckled and kept paddling.

"You can tell Sonny to shut up, but I'm not going to," I said.

"You speak Italian?"

"I'm not the uneducated fool you make me out to be."

"I never said anything about you being uneducated."

"Yeah, so tell me, Kate, have a boyfriend or two back home?"

I could see her back stiffen. Ah, I'd found a soft spot. Or sore spot. Some spot that was interesting.

I didn't intend to stop pushing either.

"I don't think that has anything to do with this trip, Mr. Wolfe."

"Why do you call me by my father's name any time there's a slight tension between us?"

"I opt for subtlety rather than the obvious."

"And the obvious being?"

Kate pointed to a rather large anteater on the side of the river, but I wasn't about to let her change the subject.

"So this is what I think, Miss Prescott."

"And what is that?" she asked, turning her head around as if she had briefly forgotten I was there.

"I think that you have a fine young man you're serious with back home. Close to being engaged, actually. I'm saying he's well off, surely good looking, probably not exactly what you dreamed of when you were younger—"

"Keep your hands out of the water!" Sonny interrupted. "I see a gator."

For a few minutes we just looked around. Then Kate reached forward to pat Sonny on the back and told him he was sweet.

I didn't see any signs of an alligator. And I'd never heard Sonny shout out like that before.

"Did I miss something?"

Sonny turned around and looked at me as though he'd like to squash me.

"I'm thinking there was no alligator," I said.

"Sonny takes the protective thing a little too literally," Kate said.

He didn't bother to turn around. "I'm thinking you might have missed him because of your big mouth."

"*Non ti preoccupare,*" she said to him, which I was pretty sure meant don't worry. Sonny didn't say anything else.

"Did I say anything—?"

"It's fine, really. I was engaged, not long ago actually."

I waited for her to explain more. I could hear Max's laugh behind us, and turned to look. The Colonel sat in my usual place, telling a story that was apparently amusing.

"How long ago?" I finally asked her.

"Weeks, actually. He ended things in a rather bad manner."

"Sorry to bring it up," I said.

Kate turned around to look at me. "You didn't know."

"Yes, but I apologize all the same."

"So in a way, Henry, all of us here are running away from our pasts, our demons. You aren't the only one."

I nodded.

It made more and more sense why Kate was out here. Probably more sense than why I was.

I heard Max's laugh again, and again I turned around. Their boat seemed to hover inches above the surface of the cloudy water. The Colonel glanced at me and waved a hand, a smile on his face. But just as he did, the grin turned into a grimace. His mouth opened and his eyes widened in alarm. I saw his hands reach for his neck.

In the tiny millisecond that the Colonel looked at me, before the screams of the natives and the shouts of our men, before everything around us turned into a bloody mess, I saw his eyes looking at me, saying one thing.

It should have been you. It should have been you.

An arrow had slammed against Colonel Cuaron's neck, surely severing one of the arteries. He had been stunned for a brief second, then reached for it. Blood gushed through his hands. His boat soon turned to chaos, as did the rest of our expedition. And all I remember was seeing the Colonel gripping at the arrow, his hands wet, his face in shock, even as he shouted words to the rest of the men, commands in Portuguese that got all their attention.

I saw Max come behind him as if to shield the Colonel from another arrow. I wanted to say *Fool, get down!*, but I had already dropped my paddle in the boat and was doing the same for Kate.

"Sonny, we got troubles!" I called out as I put an arm around her.

On either side of us were half-naked tribesmen. A flurry of arrows was coming our way.

Kate squirmed and yelled at me, but I yelled back.

"We're being attacked, stay down!"

I took out the .45 resting in the holster against my side and aimed it near the closest group of Indians. I heard a scream, a few shouts, a gunshot. I squeezed my trigger.

Nothing.

An arrow landed against our dugout, inches from where I sat. I kept trying to fire the gun.

"Safety," Kate said, her body crumpled and her face and head low, so far down she could look at me upside down.

I fumbled around and finally figured out how to undo the safety.

More shots were fired. A roaring boom shook the boat and almost knocked me out of it.

In the front of the boat, Sonny knelt, holding a shotgun in both hands. He fired off another boom that, if nothing else, surely frightened the Indians and made them think twice about standing at the edge of the river.

They were now running, not in retreat but rather keeping up with our boats.

My gun finally fired. I don't know if I hit anyone or anything, but it made itself known.

"Right side!" I heard Max's voice behind me. "Get off to the right!"

I turned and saw Max holding the Colonel in his arms. Paulo was behind him firing a rifle.

An Indian on the side of the river took a shot in the head. It wasn't a pretty picture, but I didn't have time to think or feel.

Another arrow bolted past Kate's head.

"Stay down!"

A roaring crack of the shotgun went off. Sonny was almost standing now as he fired off another round.

"Look at 'em run!"

As he laughed and cocked the shotgun, an arrow landed in his leg. He called out, laughing harder. "That the best you can do?"

He fired off another shot as I tried to do the same. More arrows zipped by.

I heard a muffled groan and looked at Sonny. Two arrows had landed in his chest.

I fired off my handgun like a madman, just firing at the Indians on one side, then the other. I was now leaning over Kate, shielding most of her body.

"Istu, get us over to the right side! Right! There—over there!"

I was pointing with my gun like a crazy man. Istu rowed and seemed undaunted by the attack.

Sonny stood up and fired off two more rounds. He shouted violently, then swayed and fell off the dugout into the shallow waters of the river.

"Sonny!" Kate said, starting to go after him.

I pulled her back. "Stop it. Get back down."

"Sonny!"

"Kate, stop it—come here—get back."

I grabbed at her and accidently pulled a clump of hair. She slapped me in my face.

"Give me a gun," she yelled.

We were approaching the shore, and the Indians for the most part had scattered. There were more on the other side of the river. I saw a rifle at Istu's feet and handed it to her.

She fired off several rounds. I saw a running native twist as he was shot in the back. Another clutched his shoulder and tripped and fell.

I couldn't see Anton's dugout, nor the fourth one with the camaradas. I turned and saw Max already on the shore, firing his handgun.

A rifle went off once, again, then again.

"Kate, stop it. Hold on there."

I grabbed her and took the rifle out of her hands. The Indians on both sides of the river had fled—those that weren't lying there dead on the praia.

Kate shook, and I held her in my arms, the .45 still in my hand.

I looked out at the water and saw the floating body of Sonny. As hard as I gripped her, I couldn't stop Kate from shivering.

H e's dead."

"Who? The Colonel or Sonny?"

"Both," Max said with a sigh. He rubbed his eyes. His hands and his face were smeared with blood.

"Where's Kate?" I asked.

"With Anton and Istu. Literally between them at camp."

"How is she?"

"Tough. And I know that some of it is bravado, but that lady is tough."

I leaned up against a massive tree. I still held the .45 in my hands. I think I might have killed an Indian with it. Unbelievably, I didn't feel any different at this reality. I was tired and nervous.

"What are we going to do?" I asked.

"Well, two camaradas were killed as well. We think another might have taken off."

"What? Where? In the jungle?"

"No. Down the river."

"With the boat?"

Max nodded. Our fourth dugout had contained most of our supplies, including valuable rations and tools.

"Oh, this is bad."

"Yes."

I laughed out of crazy, nervous energy. "I mean, this is bad."

"Listen—Anton said that we are close to the village we were heading for."

"Is it safe?"

"We're near the Tuiche River. Anton said we might want to go by foot when we reach it."

"The Colonel told me about the men's fears of the Tuiche."

Max nodded. His gray stubble made him look older.

"Do you buy into it?" I asked.

"I buy into the fact that we're strangers, and people around these parts don't necessarily like strangers."

"Yeah, I get that. But do you believe the business about it being cursed?"

"He's dead now. Maybe it is."

"Can we just pack up and head back?"

"I asked Kate if she wanted to," Max said. "She said no. She said we've gone this far."

I nodded and began picking up wood for the fire.

"Your feathers are more ruffled than hers," Max said.

"He was sitting where I should have been."

"Yes. But he asked you to change, didn't he?"

"No. I was the one who asked him. And if I hadn't . . ."

"Random, stupid luck, that's what it was," Max said. "That's what life is—one big random stream of events."

"Maybe."

"None of us knows when that time will come. The Colonel saved our lives. He knew what we needed to do, and he warned the men. He died valiantly."

"You really think so?"

"He didn't die alone," Max said. "He didn't die in vain."

"Yeah."

I didn't want to talk about it anymore. I wanted to get back to camp and be near Kate and somehow find a way to make it through the night.

Alive.

CAMP ON THE PARACATU RIVER

January 31, 1929

Just in case you've lost count, let me list the casualties.

We had barely entered the jungle, had so far left to go, and yet we had already lost too many lives on this quest in search of someone who was probably dead as well.

First there was the Colonel's right-hand man, Mateo. Perhaps that was a fluke accident, but I was beginning to think nothing was fluke and that accidents were rare around these parts.

Next came the doctor, who had a rather unfortunate meeting with a jaguar.

And now this, the sudden and violent attack on our group. Colonel Cuaron was dead, as was Sonny. Two of the camaradas were dead, another had taken the boat of supplies. This left five of them, along with Istu, Paulo, Anton, Kate, Max, and me.

I could see the remnants of our tattered group huddled around a fire even though it wasn't cold. Kate sat next to Anton, who stood when Max and I approached. Max walked over and took the Swede's place by the fire.

"How is she?" I asked him in a whisper.

"She's fine. She's okay with our plan to go to the nearby village."

"And then what?"

Anton was one of those men with few expressions. I waited to see a response from him, but none came.

"The village is half a day away. It's called Barraha."

"And after that?" I asked again.

"That will be up to Kate. This is her expedition."

"It's half gone."

He walked away to get gear and food ready for tomorrow's trek. I didn't want to get back on the water. It was a little too tainted for me.

For a moment I stared at the fire. I could see the outline of Kate's face. She laughed at something Max said, and I studied her jawline, her smile.

It was lovely, that smile. In the face of such adversity, Kate's face displayed an inner strength I didn't have. It was refreshing to see something so lovely in the middle of such a dark jungle of doubt.

I walked over to the fire and sat down.

"Anybody in the mood for campfire stories?" I asked with a smile.

Max, Kate, and I didn't want to go to sleep. Or perhaps it would be more accurate to say that we didn't want to be left alone with the night. And with our nightmares.

We had spent the last hour talking about cinema and news and prohibition and the big cities. I could tell Kate missed home.

"So tomorrow, or should I say today, since I expect it's far after midnight, is Friday," I said to Kate, who lay on her back, leaning against a couple of propped bags. "What would you be doing on this night if you were in New York?"

Kate laughed, her long hair spilling down like a waterfall. "Depends."

"Depends on what?"

"If I were there now, or if it had been a couple of months ago."

"Couple months."

"Okay, then. What would I be doing?"

"A typical Friday night for Kate Prescott."

She laughed. "There's never a typical night for her, that's for sure."

"Then pick one."

A hand stroked back hair. Women can have all the fun they want, can't they? With just a movement of their long hair, they can move a heart or stop a breath. Men can't do that. Men can't even play with their hair, or if they do they should be stopped. But ladies leisurely stroke and brush and rub their long locks, casually, nonchalantly, while the men around them stare.

Then again, maybe I was just tired and found Kate utterly beautiful because she was inches away from me, talking like a longtime friend.

"It has been fun to be a young person in her twenties during this decade. Probably a bit too much fun."

"Not you," Max said, popping in and out of our conversation as the topic interested him and as his doze waxed and waned. "Not our little God-fearing girl."

"We all have our oats to sow, don't we?"

"Well, Max is still sowing," I said.

"I used to love dancing," Kate said. "That was my favorite thing to do. Our group went to jazz clubs. All the best in town. Have you ever been to Harlem?"

"Never," Max said.

"It's amazing. The music coming out of there is utterly life changing. There are hundreds of clubs in the city with chorus lines, comedians, singers. They have it all."

"So have you been to the Cotton Club?" Max asked.

I waited to speak, biding my time.

"Yes, of course. And Connie's Inn. The Savoy, where I saw Duke Ellington. Lafayette, where I saw Bessie Smith."

"How about Ethel Waters at Connie's?"

Kate looked at me with a surprised smile. "You like Ethel Waters?"

I nodded. "It was a great show."

She waited to see if I were joking. "Stop. You were there?"

"I've been in New York many times. I do have a little culture inside of me."

"I was at that show! A couple years ago?"

I smiled at her surprise and excitement.

She shoved me with an elbow. "To think I might have passed you by. Who knows? Maybe we met that night."

"I would have remembered," I said in all honesty.

Kate started to hum, then broke out into song. *"I'll give you my love, I'm sure that love will see us through. Baby, baby, what else can I do?"* Her voice was strong, brilliant, beautiful, full of vinegar. And when she sang the word *baby*, she looked at me with a playful glance. *"If you want the moon, I'll bring the moon right down to you. Baby, baby, what else can I do?"*

"I feel I'm in the city right now," Max said.

"You can sing."

"You should see me dance," Kate said, a sparkle in her eyes.

"I want the moon," Max said.

For a few minutes Kate sang, and we listened. The tune transported us from our small campfire vigil to the city streets and night lights of the Big Apple.

I got goose bumps listening to Kate sing the Ethel Waters song. Max soon drifted off, the flicker of the fire bouncing off his rugged face.

"You have a talent," I told her.

"Thank you," she said politely. "Those were fun times."

"You say that in the past tense."

"Ever the writer, huh?"

"Why past?"

"Sometimes a girl has to grow up."

I waited for her to say more. But she wasn't giving up anything.

"Does this have something to do with your fiancé? With the breakup?"

Her eyes looked deep into the heart of the fire, lost, wandering somewhere far from where we sat. I wondered what tales she could tell, what sagas she could sing about.

"It's all one big glorious drama, that's what it has to do with. My brother and my mistakes and my fiancé—my *ex*-fiancé—my parents, the fact that I'm a woman. That always gets in the way of things. The fact that I have long legs sometimes makes matters confusing for others."

"Really? Do you think so?"

She shot me a feisty look again. The emotions of this woman could change in a heartbeat. "I know so."

"Really, because to me, they don't look all that long."

Kate didn't understand what I was talking about, then saw my smile and got the joke.

"Trust me, they're long," Kate said. "And quite attractive, if I must say."

"Yes, I think you must."

"And yes, I was living my life in New York City the way I thought it needed to be lived, the way I wanted to live it. But my brother's disappearance—it was the start of a journey for me."

"A journey that has led you to the middle of the jungle."

"Yes." She nodded. "Full of wild beasts. And animals too."

She aimed her eyes at Max, who had his mouth wide open, sleeping.

"That's true. But also full of valiant knights willing to protect and serve."

"I don't see any of those around here." She smiled at me.

"Do you miss those New York nights?"

She didn't take any time to say an immediate no. But then she thought for a few moments.

"Those nights were like beautifully colored dreams. Brilliant and bright. But that's what they were—dreams. They weren't real. I guess one morning I woke up and decided I needed to start living real life. I needed to grow up."

"Growing up is overrated," I said.

"To some. But eventually everybody needs to grow up. I guess I was forced to, but I'm glad I did."

I looked at her face and those eyes and that look and wanted to say *You're still just a girl, just a little girl dreaming and faking and acting.* But I couldn't say this. I wasn't sure how I could.

Because boys don't know how to articulate things like that.

THE VILLAGE OF BARRAHA
ALONG THE TUICHE RIVER

February 1, 1929

There was still a haze of moisture from the night of rain. We had arrived the night before and camped outside a small village on the edge of the Tuiche River several miles off of the Paracatu. Anton was the only one of our original group who could communicate with the Indians, speaking Portuguese and trying to understand their language, which had bits and pieces of Portuguese in it. Thankfully Istu was still with us and could explain what had just occurred. We'd presented the Barrahan Indians, who were known to be moderately peaceful, with several artifacts and items to please them—small things like salt and tobacco and necklaces. They had allowed us to put up our tents and sleep undisturbed.

It was morning when Anton woke me. "You need to come with me."

I followed him along the muddy riverbank to a trail leading into the jungle and the village. When I say village, I refer to a cleared-out section of the forest with small makeshift huts that seemed to barely provide cover overhead. We passed several Indians, most naked and dark-skinned. The appearance of white men wasn't shocking to them, and they greeted us with smiles and followed us.

I didn't ask Anton where we were going. I was groggy and just hoped that there was some sort of coffee waiting at the other end.

At a covered hut connected to a massive tree, Anton stopped.

"I believe this is one of the leaders of the village," he said to me before entering. "Istu told them what happened. They believe they know who attacked us and why."

I nodded. "Shouldn't Kate be here?"

"Kate is already here," I heard a voice call out from inside the hut.

I grinned at Anton, but he didn't share the glance. We entered a remarkably spacious dwelling with dry ground and flickers of light coming in from all sides of the covering made mostly of leaves.

"This is Mahaak Jehi," Anton said, gesturing toward a tall, elderly Indian clothed in a headpiece and small loincloth around his waist.

I nodded as Anton told the Indian my name. I saw Kate and Max sitting on the floor. Istu stood in the corner, almost blending in with the darkness.

"I'm not the best translator, but I'll try to sum up what the chief says."

"Is he a chief?"

"I believe he's a shaman," he said.

I could see deep lines on his dark face as Mahaak Jehi started speaking. His voice was loud, wild, almost unnerving.

"He says that you resemble another man who came here not long ago."

Kate stood up. "Anton, show him the picture." She handed him a folded photograph.

He opened it up and said a few words in Portuguese. The Indian stared at the photo intently. I wondered if it was too dark to see, but he seemed to be able to see it fine. His words seemed to confirm that it was the man.

"He's seen my brother. This means Louis made it all the way here."

I kept my doubts to myself. I'm sure Max had his own. Any white man my age might look the same to this Indian, the same way one Indian in his twenties might look the same as another to us. Kate took the picture back, and I made a mental note to ask what her brother looked like.

Anton asked us to have a seat. The Indian chief/shaman stood, speaking rapidly in a high-pitched voice. Anton would say a word here or there to try and understand, while the rest of us sat and listened. I glanced at Max, who looked at me as though he was thinking *Wish I were still in Key West.*

"He keeps referring to the jaguar attack," Anton finally said when there was a pause. "I'm not sure exactly what he's after. They hold a lot of beliefs and superstitions in the jaguar, and it seems to mean something."

"Yeah, it means that the doctor got eaten by a cat," Max said. "Nothing superstitious about that."

"Let him talk," Kate said.

"He calls it one of the seven. Something seven. Seven 'things.' I don't know. The jaguar is the first."

"Signs?" Kate asked.

"Yes, maybe. I'm not sure," Anton said.

The chief continued to talk. Occasionally Istu would say something, not asking a question but making a statement in the Indian language. Anton would nod, ask some questions, then listen.

"It sounds like he's saying guardian or protector of something. The jaguar was the first of seven guardians."

"What are they guarding?" I asked.

"I don't know. Whatever it was that Louis Prescott was looking for. The lost city, maybe."

"Do they know of a lost city?" Max asked.

"He hasn't said. The jaguar was the great lord or something like that."

"It's the Great Beast," a voice said.

We looked around and saw Istu. He stepped closer.

"The jaguar is the first of seven guardians of the holy place."

"You speak English?" Kate asked.

"I believe he does," I said.

"Since when?" Max asked. "Why the silence?"

"The Colonel spoke with you," Istu said, his square face serious, almost regal. "There was no need."

"So what is the chief saying?"

"He is encouraging us to go back. He says we have seen just the start of signs to come."

"Great," Max said.

"There is something in the wilderness, something even the

Barrahans have never seen. Something that your brother was looking for. A lost city perhaps. A temple. A place guarding the secret of eternal life."

"The Devil's Mouth?" Max asked.

Istu nodded. "The Great Beast is the first of the seven guardians, a god in the form of an animal who protects the outer rim from strangers. Then there are the actual guardians of the land, the Indians who attacked us."

"So we can expect to meet five more obstacles?" Kate asked.

Istu looked at Anton, then at the chief. Mahaak Jehi quickly spoke again, with Istu asking questions this time.

Anton tried to follow their exchange. "What was that about a snake?" he asked.

"He says there is a snake trail that heads toward the mountains," Istu said. "Then the magician."

Max laughed. "This is crazy."

"The fifth guardian is the pool of fire."

"That sounds like fun," Max said.

"Shut up," I told him.

"The walls of death are next."

"Are there any other kind?" Max said. He was obviously done with all of this, his mind either in complete disbelief or complete cynicism. "And what's after the 'walls of death'?"

"The Devil's Mouth," Istu said.

"Of course. Wonderful. Great." Max stood up. "Sign me up. I'll take a front row seat for the magician, a wade in the pool of fire, a stroll up the walls of death, and then I'll wake up with the devil."

He angrily walked out of the hut. I held up a hand to the chief as an apology. Anton tried to explain Max's actions.

"Do you believe all of this?" Kate asked Istu, then Anton.

"It's their beliefs," Anton said. "I don't know what it all means. I do know we were attacked by an animal, which I believe was just an unlucky, random event. The Indians who attacked us could have done so for any reason. There aren't many strangers that come this far down the river."

"I want to know where my brother went," Kate said. "Ask him if he saw or heard any more of my brother."

Anton asked but got nowhere. The chief seemed irritated, perhaps at the insult from Max, perhaps because of all the questioning.

"He is warning us to stay away," Istu repeated.

The chief spoke the one English word he seemed to know. He said it over and over.

"Bad. Bad. Bad."

"You still have something in that?"

Max looked at me with a mischievous grin. "Well, we are short on rations for the rest of the trip, but yes, I still have some whiskey. Want some?"

I took the worn flask. "This looks different."

"I actually brought several."

"Good to know you packed smart."

"What do you think of all this mumbo jumbo?"

"It's real. You missed it when you left."

"What?"

"The chief disappeared in a plume of smoke." I grinned.

"Great. Then did you all smoke some magic weeds?"

I laughed and looked out toward the river. The sun beamed down on it. I had no desire to get back in one of the dugouts. All of a sudden I missed Chicago, even if it was subzero back home.

I even missed Bugs Moran and his men. At least I could understand what they were saying. Now I wasn't even sure how I was going to be killed.

"Did you know that there are cannibals in these parts?" Max asked me. "Some of these Indians practice it."

"Good to know. I wonder if they've ever had a French soufflé?"

He took a swig from his flask, and I commandeered it again.

"I'm serious," Max said. "These Indians are crazy. Perhaps it's the trees and the wilderness that makes them so."

"Every faith seems crazy if you think about it. Just because they're naked and believe in sun gods doesn't make them any more insane than the crazies on Chicago street corners preaching about Jesus coming back on a horse someday."

"So you're advocating for the cannibals now, are you?" Max asked.

"I'm not advocating for anybody. I'm advocating for finding out what's in the jungle. You and I both know it might not be anything, it might all be myth."

"True. You're sounding more like me every day."

"So you don't believe any of this?"

Max shifted on the edge of the log we were sitting on. "I believe that I need to keep my gun loaded, because the further we go the more trouble we're going to find. I don't think anything's out there except skeletons and wilderness."

"But you're willing to keep going, aren't you?"

"Of course," he said. "I want to see the 'magician.' Maybe we'll get a show out of this."

"That map of yours offer any suggestions?"

Max shook his head. "I never made it this far. But this was the village we were heading to. I know that. I never knew what was beyond it."

For a few moments we sat in silence, the sounds of the jungle and the water and the life around us suddenly more apparent.

"Interesting how Istu speaks English, huh?" I said.

"Good thing for us. He almost speaks better than the Colonel."

"For some reason I don't trust him."

"I don't trust anyone out here. But he's harmless. I saw him when the Indians attacked. He was surprised."

"I'm sure we'll have a few more surprises coming."

Max nodded, then gave me the flask again.

I went back into the village to see Anton trying to consolidate the remaining rations and supplies. On the ground were boxes, clothes, and other items, including an assortment of guns.

"Where'd those come from?"

"Sonny had quite a stash."

There were two shotguns, three rifles, and five handguns.

"Why don't you take one of those?" Anton asked.

"Is a war breaking out soon?" I asked. I still had the .45 in my bag.

"Maybe." He picked up the stubby shotgun that Sonny had used, along with some cartridges. "Here. You can't miss with this."

"That would probably knock down an elephant."

"Better hope so," Anton said without a trace of humor.

I found a frantic Kate in her hut, pulling clothes out of bags and tossing them about.

"Everything okay?"

"Not now," she said without a glance in my direction.

"Can I help?"

"No." She continued looking in pockets, shaking each piece of clothing.

She wore a white shirt and remarkably clean khaki pants, and her boots were still semi-polished after all this time out here. Beads of sweat dotted her head and neck.

"I can help you look—"

"Please, Mr. Wolfe, I need to just . . ." She sat down, exhaled, and put her hands in her hair.

"What are you looking for?"

"It doesn't matter."

As she sat on the dirt floor in the small makeshift tent, her eyes still closed, I scanned the area around her. Even Kate had a gun, a small revolver.

I excused myself and stepped outside. I could see footprints leading to the edge of the jungle. Near them, on an overturned tree trunk, sat an undergarment. I went to pick it up and saw a sliver of gold slide out from the silk camisole.

On the ground glinting in the morning sun rested a necklace. A large gold heart pendant dangled against a leaf. I picked it up and smiled.

"Are you looking for this?" I called, holding the necklace in the air.

She appeared at the opening of the tent, wiped her teary eyes, and grabbed the necklace, then gave me a big hug.

"Where did you find it?"

"Along the edge of the trees on a log. You must have taken it off earlier this morning."

"I wrapped the necklace up changing this morning, then accidentally left that outside when Anton came and told me about the shaman." Kate let out a deep breath as she put the necklace back on. "Can you help?"

I fastened the lock in the back and noticed how soft and long her neck was. When she turned her head, a big grin brightened her face.

"You're something, you know that?"

"Not really," I said.

"No. You're—you're just really something."

"Okay."

"I mean, not only did you—" She touched her necklace. "My brother gave this to me. Several years ago. And he . . ."

She couldn't finish her words.

"It's fine. Really, Kate."

"No, no—wait. You didn't just come in here to find a crazy woman unraveling. But you also somehow managed to put my camisole back with my other belongings without making a scene."

I wiped my mouth, a smile on my lips. "Well, I didn't—"

"Why do you have to do things like that?"

"I'm sorry?"

"Why do you have to be so—so nice?" Kate asked. "I've given up on the male race, thank you very much. You're doing me no good acting the way you are, Henry."

"Ah, it's back to Henry, is it?"

Her eyes glowed. "Thank you."

I nodded. "It looks like Anton's almost ready to go."

"Yes. And I would be too, if it weren't for a little excursion to use the bathroom."

"Nature calls too often."

"How is Max?" she asked.

"He disbelieves everything the old Indian said, but he's keeping his gun close by just in case."

"And how are you?"

"Me? I'm fine."

She took one of my hands. "No. How are you? Really?"

"About going on?"

Kate nodded.

"Pretty much scared to death. Maybe Anton saw that in my face. I get to carry around a shotgun."

"What do you think we'll find?"

"I don't know, Kate. I really don't. But some might say it would be impossible to find a gold pendant in the middle of a jungle, right? Maybe some things are meant to be."

"Meant to be what?" Kate asked.

"Found."

ALONG THE "SNAKE'S TRAIL," HEADING TOWARD THE DOMINGAS MOUNTAIN RANGE

February 3, 1929

The Swede led us toward the mountains.

The chief had refused to provide us with directions to this lost city, but we had managed to get some help from a couple of the Indians. They confirmed Louis Prescott's roughly sketched map, according to Anton. We were to head on foot through the dense jungle toward the mountains known as the Domingas, and we would reach the lost city by connecting with a river on the other side.

We had been hiking for the last day and a half. So far the only thing ominous about the trail we were on was its beauty and serenity. The higher we went, the more picturesque everything tended to be, which made us even more anxious to see what might be lurking in the trees around us.

After a while we came upon an open field between the trees. But then the path led toward a thick jungle again. Surprisingly, there was an actual trail, apparently well traveled. The growth was dense on either side, but we could walk single file through the trees without coming across any blockage.

"So is this when we're going to see the snakes?" Max asked as he walked behind me. "Will they suddenly start coming out of the jungle?"

I was sweaty and tired. The shade felt good.

"Only when we're far enough in not to make it out alive."

"That's encouraging," Kate said, looking back at me.

Anton led our group, followed by Istu, two camaradas, then Kate. I was next, with Max, Carlos (the only camarada I knew by name), two more camaradas, and Paulo bringing up the rear. I couldn't help noticing that our numbers were getting smaller with each passing day.

The trail itself wound like a snake through the trees, as if whoever mapped this out was having a fun time weaving his way through the jungle. There was no reason for the turns; they felt like a maze, except there was only one path to follow. The trail never backtracked, but for some reason would suddenly veer right, then steer left again. Looking into the trees, we could see nothing the trail was avoiding—no massive tree or boulder or stream of running water. The path seemed to have been created by a wild child running blindly through the forest.

It was afternoon—time had disappeared just like any signs of civilization—when we decided to stop and make camp. The small trail had widened into a larger clearing in the jungle, almost a circle that opened up to the sky. Again, we weren't sure why there was suddenly a circular opening in the woods, as if it had been carefully cut out and constructed. What had it been used for? Anton searched for signs of Indians, but there were none.

"This looks like the best place to stay for the night," he said. "It might be the last bit of flat land we find for a while."

Max looked around suspiciously. "If any of those hostile Indians spot us, we're dead."

"We'll have to take shifts to watch," Anton said.

Max laughed. "Watch for what? A tribe of a hundred crazy Indians? Then what?"

"Maybe they'll be scared off by the sound of gunfire."

"And maybe it will make them angrier."

"We will not have to worry about Indians here," Istu said as he set up a tent for Kate.

"Why is that?" Max asked.

We all waited for his answer.

"This is a not a good place for them. They will not attack us, not here."

"Is this a holy place?" Kate asked.

The tall Indian shook his head. "No. It is cursed."

Those were nice words to hear as the sun slowly slipped away behind the overpowering trees.

D o you hear that?" Kate was looking up toward the open sky of a thousand distant stars.

All I could hear was the crackle of wood in the fire in front of us.

"What?"

"There. Right there. You hear that?"

"I don't hear anything."

"I know," Kate said, glancing at me. "That's just it. The complete and utter silence. Hear it?"

"Yeah."

"It's as though everything suddenly stopped. As though we're in the middle of nowhere."

"Young lady," Max said as he smoked one of his last cigarettes. "In case you didn't realize it, we've been in the middle of nowhere for some time."

"But it's never been this quiet, wouldn't you say?"

I nodded.

"Anton, I have a question for you," Kate said, looking across the fire toward the Swede, who was sharpening his large knife. "What happens if we reach this lost village, or if we reach the end of the map, and nothing's there? Either way, what happens then? What is our plan for heading home?"

He nodded as if to acknowledge the smart question. I hadn't even thought that far down the road.

"Beyond the mountains where we're headed should be a river to get us to the Tapajos River. We take that to the Amazon, then to the city of Belem."

"Long trek, is it not?" Max said.

Anton nodded.

"How long will it take?"

"It's hard to say. I can't estimate until we're on the river."

None of us wanted to say the obvious: *If we get that far.* But it was on all of our minds.

Kate was right. The silence was tangible. It was real and overpowering. The calm felt heavy, the darkness menacing. A thousand eyes surrounded us, watched us, waited for us. The fire in front of us felt as miniscule as one of those speckled dots above.

We waited for our eyes to tire. For sleep. For dawn. But this would prove to be a very long night. And we would be fortunate to live through it and see the rising sun.

I awoke with a jerk, surprised I had fallen asleep, jolted by the sound of a muffled, low-pitched groan. I had been sleeping by the fire, which throbbed with a slow, reddish burn. I couldn't see anyone else; the others had apparently gone into their tents, which were set up around the fire.

The first tent I looked at was Kate's, but it looked no different from usual. The flap was shut to keep out the mosquitoes, one of those things that was nice in theory but seldom actually worked. I could see Max's head at the front of his tent.

The groan sounded again. Now that I was standing, I could see where it was coming from. It was across the fire on the other side, between Anton's and Kate's tents.

I could see a pair of bare feet. I went closer. I thought it was Paulo, but I couldn't be sure. Something was covering his chest and face.

Snakes.

Something moved on his stomach and neck and head. Small, wiry things.

But something didn't fit. The amount of them, on top of him—something didn't look right.

"Anton," I called out.

I saw his head pop out of the tent.

"We have a problem here," I said, still a few feet away from Paulo, who shook but couldn't get out from under the snakes.

Anton bolted over to Paulo's side and wiped the snakes away from his face.

"Be careful," I said. "They might be poisonous."

Anton didn't look at me but kept pulling at something. Paulo screamed.

The Swede said something in his native tongue, something that sounded angry. He jumped back up. "Do you have a knife?" he asked me, then quickly rushed back to his tent.

Max came out from his tent. "What's going on?"

Anton re-emerged with a machete and rushed back over to Paulo as though he was going to cut off his head.

I suddenly heard Kate's voice. "Henry—what's happening?"

"Stay in your tent! Don't come out here!"

"Anton—what are you doing?" Max asked.

Anton began cutting at the writhing creatures around Paulo. "Bring me some of the fire."

I didn't understand what he meant and continued to watch in blurry slow motion as Anton hacked away at the snakes and Paulo continued to scream.

"Get another knife or something to cut with," Anton said to Max. "Henry. Fire. Quickly."

I went to our woodpile and found a stick. I pulled off my shirt, wrapped it around the stick, and lit it on fire. For a while it stayed on the piece of wood. I brought it over to Anton to give some light.

And that was when I almost fell over in disbelief.

The writhing, living creatures covering Paulo weren't snakes.

They were coiling, moving vines that seemed to be spreading the more Anton cut them. They were completely covering the Indian, pinning him down, mummifying him.

His voice screamed out again, but this time it was even more muffled.

It was muffled from the vines themselves. . . .

It can't be, not possible, not like that, not happening.

Anton kept cutting, chopping, slicing, but the vines kept growing, moving quickly like spiders, breaking apart and then suddenly slinking back together. I could see some of the leafy weeds moving up Anton's leg.

This is a dream, I thought. I'm going to wake up and find I'm dreaming.

"Henry, the fire! Use the fire."

"For what?" I asked, still not understanding.

"Light the vines on fire. Get rid of them."

Paulo's body shuddered and convulsed, and his groan sounded deep and awful.

Anton looked toward Kate's tent, still closed. He took out the gun from its holster at his side and without a thought shot the man.

I saw Kate scramble out of her tent and rush toward us, her face panicked and bewildered. I then looked at Max, who appeared as confused and shocked as I was. Anton jumped all around, stomping on the vines.

The burning shirt fell to the ground, with the vines separating from it.

They were moving. They were alive.

They acted like they—like they—

"Henry!"

Anton's scream woke me out of my trance.

I stopped standing there and got to action. Despite what I was seeing.

Despite what I was thinking.

For a few minutes, there was complete and utter terror.

I couldn't get the swirling, contorting vines out of my mind. They were exactly like snakes. And there were hundreds of them, perhaps all linked and coiled together. I felt surrounded. And smothered. And suffocated.

I heard some shouts. Two camaradas were nearby, flailing at the ground with their legs. Several others had taken off in complete hysteria. Kate was yelling—Max went to her. I couldn't see Istu.

I threw some branches into the fire, then tossed a few heavy chunks of wood on top. Then I took a long leafy branch in my hand and lit it on fire. It took a couple of minutes but soon it was burning fast and bright.

I took it over to Anton, who was dripping with sweat as he swung his machete furiously. He looked like a man possessed.

Which he was, I decided. He had just shot a man who was being suffocated by vines.

Yeah, I'd probably look that way too. Maybe I did.

For a second, I looked down at Paulo. Vines were wrapped around his body, especially his neck. And I could see them going into his mouth.

"Here, give me that," Anton said. "Get more. Bring more."

Anton took the branch and set it on the vines. Some of them lit and turned black as they fizzled out. The patch around the burning branch suddenly was clear. Unlike the rest of the ground all around us.

I suddenly noticed that I was standing on these vines. They encompassed our entire campsite. All around our tents, everywhere. Everywhere except for around the fire.

Now I could see Anton's logic.

They moved like snakes. I rushed to the fire and did the same thing with another branch, setting it ablaze and then coming back out and giving it to him. He would go around and light some of the vines on fire, making it spread and move like retreating reptiles.

"Where's Istu?" he asked me.

"I don't know," I said, going back to the fire.

"Max? Hey, Max, are you okay?" Anton called.

"Yes."

"Go back in the tent and stay with Kate."

"I don't know if we should do that."

We looked back at Max and Kate who stood near the fire.

"Those—those things—have gotten in the tents."

"Then help us with the fire. We need to make a big ring around our site. Make sure we keep those things out."

I looked at the trees that surrounded us. And I recalled Istu's words.

This place is cursed.

I found it interesting that the man who'd said this was nowhere to be found.

Kate cried out.

I darted over to her with the machete I'd taken from Anton and chopped the moving things around her. We picked vines by the handful and threw them into the fire.

"Sorry—I just—they move so fast—it's creepy. And I don't want to touch them."

Max and Anton had almost lit an entire circle of fire around our campsite. Istu had suddenly turned up and was helping out. One of the other camaradas had run off into the jungle in fear. My job was staying near Kate and taking whatever vines were in our camp and burning them.

They smelled odd as they burned to a black crisp. It was a strange peppery sort of smell.

"There—right there," Kate said.

I hacked away and continued stoking the fire. My forehead and face and bare chest were wet with sweat. At one point I glanced at Kate, who smiled at me.

I wiped my face with my forearm and politely smiled back.

Things just kept getting stranger. But then again, I was strangely okay with that.

The flames crackled all around us. Within the fiery perimeter we could breathe, but the area didn't allow for much air and certainly not for peace of mind. We had taken the tents down in fear of their burning, and piled everything in one big heap that we huddled around. Kate rested against a sleeping bag, dozing. Max sat next to her, smoking, his eyes glassy and the lines under them heavy and deep. Anton and I stood watch.

Stood watch. What a ridiculous statement. We were guarding ourselves from vines. Mysterious, evil vines. It sounds preposterous; even at the time it felt beyond believable. Yet I had seen them surround and smother the Indian named Paulo. That was real. And when you witness a death (an occurrence all too familiar on this ill-fated trip), you tend to be willing to believe anything.

Anton came beside me, his forehead smeared with sweat and dirt and ash. He gritted his teeth and stared around at the darkness beyond the flames.

"Ever seen anything like this before?" I asked.

I expected perhaps *When I was in the Philippines* or perhaps even *A sherpa once told me . . .* but Anton only shook his head.

"No."

"That's comforting," I said, trying for a little levity.

"Then again, I've never been somewhere this remote."

"It's almost as if they have a life of their own."

"Vines are alive, but I've never seen anything like that. Doesn't the Frenchman know about plants and animals?"

I looked back at Max, who seemed to be asleep, even though a cigarette still stuck out of his mouth.

"He used to know a lot. But I doubt he's seen anything like this before."

Anton let out a sigh.

"The map that Louis made—does it show any of this?"

Anton glanced at me, for a second unsure whether to take out the map that he guarded so carefully. But this far into the trip, into the madness in which we found ourselves, such precautions appeared irrelevant. He took out a folded piece of paper and opened it up, making sure he had enough light to read it. For a few moments, he studied it.

"It shows curly shapes that I assume are snakes. Louis put an exclamation point next to it, nothing more. I think he wrote notes to go with the map, but they were lost."

"But we're still headed in the right direction?"

Anton nodded. "He was here. This path heads up the mountain to a canyon. Beyond the mountains, a river will take us to the end."

I laughed. "The end. We've come all this way searching for 'the end.'"

"It's not known what we will find. But there will be something."

"And when we get there, then what?"

He looked at me, his square face strangely absent of emotion. "My job is to get us there. And to see if Kate's brother is alive."

"How far does the map show he got?"

"It stops once he reached the river beyond. Perhaps what they call the pool of fire, or perhaps the Devil's Mouth. But beyond this mountain is the last place he is known to have reached."

Looking out in the fire engulfed by darkness, I just hoped it wouldn't be the last place we reached as well.

APPROACHING THE MAGICIAN
(THE DOMINGAS MOUNTAINS)

February 5, 1929

Take a third-person, omniscient view for a moment.

The determined, strapping (love that word, strapping) blond in khakis and a black, worn captain's cap often walked too fast before having to stop or slow down. He guided the others up the mountain, which had not become less dense of trees and vegetation. They headed toward two peaks in the distance.

A lean Frenchman followed, seemingly uninterested in his surroundings but more perceptive than a casual observer would guess. His suit coat was dirty, his fedora worn and weathered. They fit in well with his face and deep-set, brooding eyes.

A woman followed, beautiful in spite of her dirtiness, full of life despite the death surrounding them. Remarkably, her brown pants and white shirt looked almost new, and her hair looked washed. She breathed heavily from exhaustion, more noticeably than the men, but she didn't draw attention to it.

The scruffy man with the shotgun sticking out from his bag (that'd be me) followed close behind the woman, sometimes by her side, talking, laughing, trying to forget the ache in his legs and side or the pure fatigue he carried. His boots were full of dark soot, his pants were torn, his black hat smelled of smoke.

Behind them were the two remaining camaradas, with Istu carrying the most and bringing up the rear.

Seven left.

Headed upwards toward an increasingly steep mountain.

On their way to meet something or someone called The Magician.

The skies above were getting dark, though it was only the middle of the day.

We walked along the edge of a hill toward the two mountain peaks. The trail was clear; there was ground beneath our feet instead of grass and weeds. I couldn't help looking around for more of those demon weeds, as I called them. But none could be found.

Something else, however, was found. Something even worse than the demon weeds.

Max was the first to spot it. He stopped and acted as though he was lighting a cigarette (and by now you might be wondering how many he had taken along—he must have found another pack). He urged Kate to go on, then pointed his head toward a small rise in the ground just to the right of our path.

I saw it at once, and was thankful Kate had not.

"We're definitely on the right path," Max said, quickly adding "to a quick death."

There was a long stake in the ground, with a small round unmistakable object attached to the top.

"I've never seen a real one," I said.

The head was truly shrunken, with the nose and mouth jutting outwards like some strange, twisted animal. Long strings hung out of the wide mouth and equally long hair fell down behind it.

"You know how they do that?" Max said.

"Not really. The question for me is why?"

"Matters of the spirit, my dear Watson. They think that they can harness the spirits of their enemies by shrinking their head."

"Who needs to harness anything when your head looks like that?"

Istu caught up with us then. He looked at the head but made no remark; he just walked on.

"Perhaps he knew this man," Max said with a smile.

"Could've been a woman."

"They say they remove a skull from the victim's head by cutting on the back of the neck and removing the flesh from the cranium."

"I just love your encouraging stories," I said as I started on up the trail, away from the shrunken head.

"The eyes are sewn shut, and then they fasten the mouth with splinters."

"Your college education was invaluable."

"The fat is taken out of the head and the flesh is boiled in water, then dried and shaped to resemble a head."

"Speaking from experience?" I asked, not overly interested in hearing about something that could actually happen to one of us.

Ten minutes later, Kate saw one.

"That's a shrunken head!" she said in horror.

"Maybe they're just smaller out here in these parts," I said.

She rolled her eyes. "What's that mean?"

"I think it's a welcome sign. We have mats, they have shrunken heads."

Max chimed in. "It's to prevent their enemies from avenging their deaths."

"Doesn't look like this poor fella is going to avenge anything," Kate said.

I smiled, glad to see Kate's humor. We were all a bit tired and slaphappy. "And you know, he's never going to have a headache."

Kate played along. "Perhaps it's good for the skin, too."

"Smooths out the wrinkles," I said. "Max is thinking about getting one."

"I've already had a couple," he said. "They're good for the soul. You suddenly lose every train of thought you've ever had."

Up ahead of us, Anton stopped. He held up a hand. "See that in the distance?"

The mountain grew steep and rocky. The sides were straight and smooth, impossible to climb. We could see a narrow canyon slicing the large barrier in front of us.

Something stood in front of the opening to the narrow passageway.

"What is that?" Kate asked.

"It looks like a wall—or some sort of gate."

"It must be pretty big if we can see it from all the way down here," I said.

And in another hour of walking, we would discover that I was partially right.

It wasn't pretty at all, but it was certainly big.

In fact, it was an immense wall that looked impossible to get through. Or over.

We couldn't help stepping over the bones. They were everywhere. If they were anything more than animal bones, I didn't want to know it. They crunched under our shoes as we approached the ten-foot wall. It was made of tree trunks bound together with vines and stood at the entrance to the canyon. On either side of us, the rocky mountain stood thirty or forty feet above us. The canyon path seemed to ascend into the hills.

"What now?" Kate asked.

Anton consulted his map. "There's a wall drawn in here. The path leads on up. Somehow he got through this."

There didn't seem to be any sort of door or opening. The logs were too smooth to climb over.

"Do we have any rope?" Kate asked.

"It was with the supplies on the dugout the camarada took," Anton said.

"Any suggestions, Istu?" I asked.

The Indian looked nervous. "We should not go beyond this gate."

"It's a gate?" Max asked. "That means we can get through it."

Istu didn't look at Max. He stared at me. "This place is cursed."

"You said that about the vines," I said. "And you were strangely absent when they attacked."

"Many men have died here."

"I doubt many men have even been here," Max said, kneeling and looking at the bones. "These are not bones of men."

"Whatever they're the bones of, it's something that died."

"This place is full of death," Istu said.

"Stop with the ominous talk," Max said.

A gust of wind blew against us, and for a moment we all stopped and looked up.

The sky grew darker.

"Anton, is there any way to get through that?" I called out over the howl of the wind.

"I can't see one." He was on his hands and knees, looking underneath the wooden beams, shaking them.

A high-pitched wail made us all stop and look around. It was a scream that was louder than the wind, higher, and scarier.

Kate let out a cry as she pointed up the cliff. At the top stood a dark-skinned man, naked except for a small cloth around his waist. He looked bony and muscular at the same time. And he looked old. Very old. He stood with raised hands toward the sky and continued to howl.

"Oh, this can't be good," Max said.

I heard steps running away from us—bolting in fact—and

thought it was Istu. Instead, I saw our camaradas bolting down the hill and back where we had come from.

"Stay here!" I called out to Istu.

He stood there, not surprised, not alarmed, no emotion at all.

"What's he doing?" Kate asked.

"He's going to turn himself into an eagle," Max said.

I felt a raindrop. And for a second I wondered . . . but of course, I knew it was impossible. A man can't make it rain. It was already cloudy. Sure, it had turned cloudy suddenly, but they didn't call this the rainforest for nothing.

Suddenly the rain unloaded onto all of us. It didn't just start pouring. It was gushing down.

Kate stood with her mouth open, her hair already soaked, her face muddy from dirty hands wiping away her long locks.

"Can we get through it?" I asked Anton.

He ignored me and kept studying the wall. The droplets were colossal, and the ground around us was already soaked. The baying of the Indian man above us continued. He wasn't singing, wasn't speaking, but whatever he was doing seemed to make sense to him. His yells were short, choppy, like a violently crazy person calling out "Yeeyeeyee!"

"What's going on?" I asked Istu.

"He is calling on the god of the dead ones to come avenge their deaths."

"What?" Max asked. "We had nothing to do with them!"

"The rain falls down with vengeance," Istu said.

I looked at my boots and could see water running over the top of them.

Rainwater was not only coming from above us, but from the small canyon between the mountains.

I saw Anton using his machete on the wood of the gate. He didn't say anything, didn't ask for help, simply starting hacking away.

This went on for a few minutes. Ten, fifteen, I don't know. I was cold from the rain and tried to shield Kate from it. Of course this was impossible, but it was my attempt at chivalry. Max continued watching both the possessed Indian above us and Istu, skeptical of both. At one point Anton slipped into the stream of muddy water he was straddling. He fell on his side, his face and hair and body covered in mud. I called out to ask if he wanted help, but he shook his head and waved a hand to let us know he was okay.

The rain fell harder. The more the Indian above us shrieked, the harder the rain fell.

"Make him stop," Kate said to me.

I was holding her now, her body shivering, her hair stuck against her cheek, against her lips.

"Please make him stop."

"It'll be okay. He's not making it rain."

As if on cue the voice changed, sounding amazingly louder, stranger, deeper. And with that suddenly came colder rain, fists of hail. One struck my head. It felt like a baseball.

"Kate, get on your knees."

She did as I asked as we hovered next to a wall. I covered her head and body with my own. Rushing water came up to our ankles. The hail seemed sporadic, falling in large clumps, then stopping, then unleashing itself again, like a flurry of hard snowballs thrown by a group of thugs.

I looked over and saw that Anton seemed to be making some headway in cutting into the wood. But I wasn't sure how he was going to get an opening big enough for us to fit through.

"Henry!" Max shouted. "Look up there."

From where I sat I could no longer see the crazy man. The hail had stopped, but the rain continued to fall.

"We have to get out of here," I said to him.

The water was now up to my knees. It made no sense how it could be raining this hard, how the waters could have risen this quickly.

"Look at the medicine man up there."

From where I stood, it looked like something was on fire. The sky was dark, and all around us was rain and fog from clouds. But above the Indian—something seemed to burn.

"What is that?"

Istu said something in his Indian language.

Max took out his pistol.

"What are you going to do with that?"

"I'm waiting to see what *he's* going to do with *that*."

It looked as though a ball of fire hovered above the Indian's hands.

This was crazy, of course. And why they called this man the magician. He wasn't *making* it rain. He hadn't *created* a ball of fire. He was high above us, and we couldn't see him all that well.

Something flung into the side canyon next to us. Chunks of rock and mud and dirt exploded everywhere. Max shouted, and Anton stopped what he was doing. Kate stood up to see what was happening. I took out my shotgun.

This time we saw it coming. A blast of fire came rolling down toward us and exploded.

All I could think was *This is not really happening this is impossible,* but it was happening and I could taste the rain and the mud and now I could smell the smoke from the ball of fire.

Anton raised his rifle and fired off a couple of shots. The howling above stopped, but I couldn't see what had happened.

"Did you get him?" I asked, looking up.

We were all looking up when Anton got stabbed in the side.

He didn't scream or even cry out. But he did manage to fire off a couple shots.

When we actually looked over to see what had happened, it was a blur of motion in an already blurry condition.

What we saw was Istu pulling a blade out of Anton's gut. Anton shoved Istu back and aimed the rifle at him. But as the gun fired, it was Anton who fell back in blinding pain. Istu ran off.

In an instant Kate was by Anton's side. "Are you okay? Anton, what happened?"

Max held his gun and kept looking up, then back down the hill where Istu had disappeared.

For a brief second amidst the steady stream of rain, I shared a glance with Max that both of us understood.

The last time I saw that look was in Egypt.

It was the look of a man who questioned whether he and his

friends would survive another day. A man who was contemplating his mortality.

I looked away and went to help Kate remove Anton's shirt.

The Swede was muscular and didn't have a hair on his body. His cut was deep, and the blood flowed like rain. We took out a shirt and held it against the cut, then Kate got some bandages and did a quick job of covering up the wound.

"We'll need to stitch it up when we can, but not here," she said.

Anton gritted his teeth. "Keep hacking at the wall—I almost cut through several of the binds. They wove it through the logs—if you cut it away I have a feeling they will move."

I nodded and got his machete.

"Tell Max to keep guard. Give him your shotgun."

I nodded. "Kate—?"

"I'm fine."

I nodded and started cutting. It felt as though it had been raining for hours, but in fact it had probably only been thirty minutes.

The rainwaters still came up to our knees.

We needed to get out of there.

T he skies are clearing off."

Max pointed as he led us up the narrow ascent. It had been fifteen minutes or more since the rope on the logs had been sliced and we'd been able to squeeze through the wall. For a while the rock walls beside us remained thirty or forty feet tall, but as the path ascended the walls grew shorter. Kate walked next to Anton, providing support if he needed it. He held the shirt firmly against his side, the cloth bloody and damp in his muddy hand. The rain had stopped, and we were nearing the end of the canyon, which I assumed would be the top of the mountain.

"I hope the 'magician' isn't waiting for us up there," I said.

"Or Istu," Max replied.

"You okay, Anton?" I checked.

He nodded, his jaw firm, his breathing heavy.

I knew that when we got to the top of the mountain we would need to dress the wound.

As we walked over rocks, Anton stumbled, and Kate helped him regain his footing. I went toward them.

"I'm fine," Anton said. "I'm okay."

He didn't look fine or okay, and the look in Kate's eyes told me the same thing. He looked pale and tired, and the look in his eyes wasn't good.

"Come on then," Max said. "Just a little farther."

The rocky terrain started to become more green and lush, with trees and bushes sprouting on the sides of the canyon. Anton needed to stop every ten minutes, drink some water, sit down. It was good to finally hear Max say, "I'm at the top."

But before we could join him and celebrate, he turned back toward us with an amused chuckle. "We've got a problem."

ON THE MOUNTAIN PEAK

February 5, 1929

Max and I stood at the edge of the cliff, peering out over the beautiful panorama. At another time we would have enjoyed the lush scenery and the afternoon glow. But now all we could think about was our way out, off this mountaintop and out of the jungle.

"How far down you think that is?" I asked him.

"Far enough to break your neck. Or your legs. Or your spine."

"The water will soften the fall."

Max laughed. "If you make it into the river. There's lots of dry spots around."

The river below us looked narrow and quick flowing. There didn't seem to be any jutting rocks in the water itself, from where we could see, but rocks were everywhere else.

"How deep do you think it is?"

"Could be twenty feet or could be two."

"You're not very optimistic," I told him.

"Look—some Indian shaman just shot fireballs at us. And unleashed the skies around us. And then there's Istu," Max yelled.

"Wonder where he went."

"Probably to get reinforcements," Max said. "We can't go back the way we came."

"Can we climb down this wall?"

The smooth, sharp edge of the mountain went straight down. Max didn't bother answering.

"Any ideas then?" I asked.

"Yes. Of course. You jump first."

"Me? Why me?"

"You're younger."

"Yeah, and that means I have more life to live. You've already lived long enough. Give us younger kids a chance to have what you had."

"The fall alone might kill me," Max said. "My heart. It's fragile."

I laughed. "Since when do you have a heart?"

"Then my kidneys."

Kate walked up beside us.

"Anton's dressing isn't going to hold for long. He's still bleeding heavily."

He was sitting on a rock in the shade, resting.

"Any prospects?" Kate asked.

"Yes," Max said. "Henry has volunteered to jump first."

"Actually, I tried to, but Max is insisting on going himself."

Kate looked over the edge of the mountain, then back at the path we had just come up. "If we go back down, we might not be able to make it around this mountain," she said. "We might not be able to find the river again."

"And we might not be alive if we try and jump," Max said to her.

"What other options are there?" she asked.

Neither Max nor I spoke for a moment.

"There's my answer then."

"What?"

She was standing a little too close to the edge of the mountain. I pulled at her arm, and she snapped her head back and shot me a look.

"I just don't want you to fall," I said.

"I'm fine."

"I know, but—"

"You can let go of me now," Kate said.

I hadn't been aware that I was still holding on to her.

"It's obvious what we need to do," she said. "This is a leap of faith."

"It's a foolish leap," Max said. "No need to risk our lives to get to that river."

"Then what do we do? Go back?"

Max nodded. "That's my suggestion."

Kate nodded, pulling her hair back in a ponytail. She glanced at me, her face registering annoyance and exhaustion. "And you?"

"What?" I asked.

"What's your 'suggestion'?"

"I don't know."

Kate muttered something as she walked away to speak to Anton. In a few minutes she came back with her pack in one hand. She slipped it over her shoulder.

"You two make a good team," she said. "I don't know which quality I find more endearing. Fear. Or indecison."

Max raised his eyebrows, amused.

"Look, Kate, all we're saying is that—"

But before I could finish my sentence, she was gone.

And before we could even get to the edge of the mountain, we heard a splash from below.

I felt panicked and sick. I stepped cautiously onto the rocky ledge, and as I took in a deep breath I heard a howl of laughter from below.

"Come on, little boys! The water's warm."

I jumped last.

My heart was still beating fast from watching Kate casually fling herself over the side of the mountain.

I was not used to a woman like Kate. Never in my life had I met someone who would literally jump off a cliff without a thought.

I wondered if it was love for her brother that drove her to such brave (and rash) actions. Or was it her faith that gave her some kind of unique threshold for fear? All I knew was that after watching Anton and Max drop down to the water below, I felt a panic, wondering if I could do it.

The three of them had floated downstream and waited for me.

Max called out something, but I couldn't hear him.

What if I hit a rock? None of them had, but it was still possible. What if I landed in a shallow portion the others hadn't found?

"Come on, Henry!" Kate's voice echoed.

And I realized I wasn't scared of falling. I was still getting over the fear I'd had watching her fall.

It was at that strange moment, after having experienced a hundred different crazy events along this journey, that the craziest thing yet happened. Kate's face, her smile, her long hair, her voice, her laugh—all of these and more ran through my mind.

I had nothing to fear. I'd already fallen.

The river we dropped into opened up into a round lake surrounded by mountains on one side and jungle on the other. The bright afternoon sun beamed on the water, illuminating the surface and everything around it. The warm glow seemed to capture our mood and the moment.

Across the lake was a wide shore that we were swimming toward. We decided to head there in order to let all of our belongings dry, then follow the river on foot.

Kate was swimming slowly in the middle of the lake. She pulled the pack over her shoulder. I swam up next to her.

"Need help?"

"No, I'm fine."

"Of course you are," I said, drifting in the water.

"What's that mean?"

"Oh, nothing."

"It means something. Otherwise you wouldn't have said it."

"I've never met anyone like you."

"Do you mean you've never met a woman like me?" Kate asked, her face and hair wet, her forehead shiny from the sun.

"Yeah, probably."

"That's what my brother always said. One of a kind. That's me."

"You could've been killed," I told her.

"And you could have been killed any number of times. When you covered me from those—whatever those balls of fire were. We all could've been killed."

"But what you did was brave."

"It was crazy," she admitted.

"Well, yeah, that too."

"Afraid?"

I looked at her for a moment, her face and her eyes and her lips so close to my own. "Afraid of what?"

"Me."

I loved the smile covering her face. It was wild and free and utterly enticing.

Just as I was going to reply with a witty retort, Max called out to us.

"Hey—not that I want to interrupt a romantic moment, but we've got a problem."

"That's all you're good at saying," I said back to him.

"We have to get out of this lake."

"Why?" I was in no rush.

"Because we have little guests."

"What?" Kate asked, swimming toward Max.

We were in the center of the lake. Anton slowly paddled his way toward us, his wound surely making it more difficult to proceed.

"There are piranha here. *Lots* of them."

As I swam closer to Max, I could suddenly see them. And feel them around me.

It was like a massive swarm of vibrating fish.

"They're not supposed to attack, are they?" I asked as I went toward Kate to get her pack.

"No. They don't attack unless they taste blood."

We all turned to look at Anton, who was swimming toward us.

Out tranquil interlude in the lake was over.

IN THE LAKE

February 5, 1929

For a second, all of us remained where we were, floating on the surface of the clear lake, treading water, our gazes capturing what we all felt. Fear, panic, desperation. But Anton looked like he always did. Calm, serious, in control.

"Anton," I called out to him. "You gotta get out of here."

"Get Kate out of the water," he said.

I didn't want to move. I could feel the fish against my legs, gliding by my chest, hitting my arms. Moving might mean that they would bite.

"You have to—"

"Henry! Get Kate out of here!"

I grabbed for Kate's hand and started swimming toward the

shore. Kate did the same, pulling her hand away from mine and using it to propel herself. I didn't breathe as I swam toward land. I could feel a burning sensation on my leg—was it bitten? Was it my imagination?

Suddenly I thought of Max.

He was still out there by Anton.

"Max!" I called out.

"Get out of here, Henry."

Kate was still swimming. I felt torn.

But there was nothing I could do. What felt like hundreds of swimming, living creatures surrounded me.

Was he sure they were piranha? I could hear him talking to Anton.

"Max, come on."

Then Anton screamed.

He was not the type to scream.

I began to paddle furiously, propelling myself with my hands and my legs to get out and make sure Kate was out too.

The screaming continued.

On shore, Kate stood and shivered, not from the cold but from fear. I finally reached her, wiping my eyes clear. The screams were terrifying now, the sound of a man being tortured.

"Kate, don't, please—" I tried to shield her, to hug her.

"No. No. Leave me alone!"

She turned her tear-filled face out to the lake, and I did the same.

Anton was flailing and splashing around like a man possessed. The piranha, hundreds of them, were attacking him. I saw one fish actually jump out of the water in its bloodthirsty madness.

Anton was screaming and sucking in water and trying uselessly to fight them off.

Max was halfway between us and Anton. He paused again, turning around.

"Max, get out of the water!" I said to him. "Get out of there!"

Anton went under, then rushed to the surface. He raised an arm, and I could see the piranha attached to it, blood and water all mixed together. His cries were high and frantic.

I tried again. "Kate, don't."

I felt so powerless.

Max was swimming toward us now. He reached us and stepped out of the water. On his face was something unfamiliar and terrifying.

Tears.

He fell to his knees, weeping, murmuring something in French.

I could see Anton looking at us, a face in terror and pain, a bloody hand reaching out toward us.

And then the cries and the flailing were over.

Anton was gone.

The piranha were surely still dining on him as his body fell to the bottom of the lake.

Max stood up and walked toward the edge of the jungle. I looked at Kate.

"I'm sorry," was all I could tell her.

"There was nothing I could do," she said.

"What?"

"That's what Max said. 'There was nothing I could do.' "

"There was nothing any of us could do."

Kate looked desperate. "I'm the one who jumped into the water. I'm the one who brought us to this point. Everything—all of this— is my fault."

"Kate—"

"Don't, please. I don't need a hug, and I surely don't need sympathy. I need honesty. That man's death is my fault."

"You couldn't help it."

"We're all going to die out here, Henry. I suggest you get on your knees and pray."

"I don't pray."

Kate didn't look scared. She looked—was it possible—almost delirious.

"Pray-er or not, we're all going to be meeting our Maker," Kate said. "You just might want to introduce yourself before you get there."

CAMP ALONG THE RIVER

Did you hear that?"

Kate and Max looked at me. Both of them looked tired and defeated, in no mood for conversation.

I wondered if I looked the same.

"Hear what?" Max asked, the glow of the fire moving across his face.

"A rustling in the woods."

Kate shook her head. "It can only be one of ten things. A jaguar. Or an Indian headhunter. Or maybe a witch doctor. Or how about a talking, walking piranha." Her voice sounded angry and giddy at the same time.

We had not spoken about Anton's death. There wasn't much

point. We had walked upriver for a while simply to get some distance from the lake and the picture we had witnessed earlier. We eventually found an appropriate sandbank to camp on. Max had gone out on his own and brought back a mutum, a kind of wild turkey, that he'd managed to find and shoot. Normally this would be a cause of celebration, but we all seemed to feel we deserved this. The gods had been cruel to us; they owed us something, anything, and this wild bird was it.

But even on full stomachs, we didn't feel satisfied.

"It sounded like footsteps," I said.

We were all holding guns, including Kate. I had my shotgun at my feet, while Max had his rifle in his hands. Earlier that evening, we had cleaned and dried the weapons to make sure they still worked properly after taking a swim in the river.

We were getting used to this gun-toting mentality.

"Tell me, Kate," Max said as he stared into the fire. "Does your God forgive stupidity?"

I could see Kate's full lips tighten. "I can't say. I can't say anything. All I know is that I'm pretty angry at him."

"I remember feeling like that. Angry. But you grow disenchanted when the anger falls on deaf ears. When there's nowhere to go with it."

"I'm not having a crisis of faith, Max."

"Then what are you experiencing?"

"I'm tired," Kate said. "And I'm worn out trying to know if I should be here in the first place. What is God's will? Did God want me to come out here? To come out here and die? Probably not. Does he care? Yes, I believe so. Is he watching over us? I think he is."

"But we're on our own," Max said. "He's watching, but he's apparently not going to get involved."

"Maybe. But he can. I have to believe he can be involved, that he can help out if we need him, that he can show his face in the darkest of places."

"Kate, please," I finally said.

"What?"

"For such a strong will, you sure are putting a lot of trust in something that isn't there."

"I battle with my will every day. We all do."

Normally I would be witty, provide some levity, but it didn't belong there in our conversation. I wasn't sure what to say.

For a while none of us said much.

"Henry?"

"Yes?"

"What are you looking for?"

For a moment I stared into the fire, my body tired and my mind weary. It was a good question. One I never asked myself.

"I don't think I'm looking for anything. I spend too much time running away and looking over my shoulder to try and see what's ahead."

Kate nodded, a grin appearing on her face.

"What?"

"For someone who tries his hardest to act nonchalant and shallow of heart, you are a deep person."

Max laughed at this. "Don't let him fool you, dear. He really isn't."

"Max is right for once," I added. "I'm really not."

"You might be foolhardy and might take life as an interesting anecdote, but you are deep, Henry Wolfe. This I know."

"Deep or not, I'm tired, yet I'm not sleeping a wink tonight. I know I heard something. I don't trust what's out there. God or not."

It was a long night.

Max didn't sleep much either. He would occasionally stand up, walk around the campfire, go to the edge of the water, come back and sit down, doze off for a few moments, wake up and have a cigarette, doze off again. Kate lay in between us, covered by a blanket. We no longer had any tents—they had disappeared with one of the camaradas. Somehow she looked peaceful in her sleep, but perhaps this was just an illusion the fire and the jungle and the night were playing with my eyes.

I could hear her question: *What are you looking for?*

It was a good question, even though I had no answer.

I believed that there were people who spent their whole lives desperately searching for something, for meaning, for hope, but I was not one of those. I was interested in what was around the corner, what was behind the door, what was inside the hole, what was hidden inside the vault. My life was one of questions, with very few answers.

Even when presented with life's tough choices and lessons, I just kept walking. The choices and lessons could be contemplated by others. I simply wanted to keep moving. Keep searching. Keep questioning.

This was why I enjoyed my relationship with Max. He didn't probe and didn't preach. He was a lot like me in some ways. Older and more cynical, sure. And he believed in more. But his faith was one of lost love. I never had the faith to begin with.

Kate stirred in her sleep. She was so beautiful. I couldn't help wishing I could be close to her, in her arms. Simply resting with her. At peace.

Peace.

That would be nice. That was something. Peace. Peace at last. Being at rest and feeling okay with that.

My whole life had been spent running. Running away and running toward.

Peace was not something I was good at.

And it was something I believed was impossible to find.

*P*eace might not have come, but sleep did.

For a very short while. I wasn't sure how long.

All I know is that in the few minutes I had dozed off, I heard footsteps. A crackling of a branch, a brush of a bush.

Something woke me up.

I knew I heard it. I wasn't dreaming.

I stood and faced the dark jungle with my shotgun.

There could be a hundred Indians waiting to attack.

A hundred. Or a thousand.

This far in the rainforest, these Indians probably had never seen other humans. Especially white people.

The burning embers of the fire illuminated Kate and Max where they slept. I remained quiet to let them continue to dream.

I waited.

And waited.

And I heard nothing else.

But someone was out there.

Someone. Or something.

I rinsed my face in the river and was coming back to camp when Kate stood, looking vibrant and refreshed.

What a vision.

A man could grow used to waking up beside a face like that. Beside a spirit like that.

"I have some good news," she said to Max and me.

"You weren't devoured by flesh-eating piranha," Max said, his morning mood not quite similar to Kate's.

"That too. But I have to show you something."

She produced a document. "This is the map that I gave to Anton. Somehow he managed to give it back to me."

"Can I see that?" Max asked. "I think there's still a chance I can burn that thing."

"When did he give it back to you?"

"He must have slipped it in my bag before I jumped," Kate told me. "At least we still have some direction."

"We still have the Devil's Mouth to look forward to," Max said.

"Hush. Someone woke up on the wrong side of the bed today."

Max laughed. "I woke up on the wrong side of the country. I should be back in Rio."

"So where does the map have us heading next?"

"Do you want to take over navigating?"

I waved my hands up. "No thanks. It seems like that's something Max can do."

"Seems like people who do that end up dying," Max said.

"Fine," Kate said. "I'll do it. But then you have to listen to my orders."

"Haven't we been doing that for the last week?" I asked.

"Funny."

"So what's next?"

"Some type of cliffs."

"The 'walls of death.' Don't you remember?"

"I thought you didn't believe in any of that," Kate said to me.

"I have no idea what I believe or don't believe. At this point, if people came flying down with wings and took us away, I wouldn't be surprised."

IN THE MIDDLE OF NOWHERE
(STILL ALONG THE RIVER)

February 6, 1929

Our new leader was easy to follow. I'd probably follow her over a cliff.

In fact, I just had.

We spent the morning walking alongside the river. Kate led, and she did so with a fire that had suddenly seemed to ignite upon learning she had the map. A couple times Max and I asked her to slow down.

The river wound its way through the jungle. We could see another set of mountains in the distance. Ideally we would have been traveling by dugout, but since it was just us three and our legs and the small amount of belongings we still had, we had to pace ourselves.

The day was hot, and we were wet with sweat. I can still see Kate opening a button on her wrinkled and muddy shirt to reveal a damp neck that she wiped with her hand. Despite the fact that her hair was wildly matted and her clothes ruined, she glowed. Max and I looked tired and worn and haggard, but Kate looked radiant.

Perhaps this was the heat and exhaustion taking hold, but I doubted it. I knew what I saw.

Occasionally, our route along the edge of the river would become thick with brush and wild growth, forcing us back into the jungle to find a more manageable path ahead. Sometimes this wouldn't work, and all we could do was take turns hacking away with the machete. It took several hours to go even a small distance down the river.

Near midday we were searching for an appropriate place to stop and rest. We doubted there would be anything to eat for lunch, but we could still try.

We had just circled into the jungle because the river had grown wild with rapids, and we couldn't walk alongside it due to impenetrable rocks and trees. The tree cover in the jungle kept us out of the sun but still made us sweat from the stifling temperature and humidity.

Kate had found an opening to what looked like a large sandbank.

"You're not going to believe this," she said as we followed her through a field of thick, knee-high grass and felt the sun on our foreheads.

"What?"

"Those are dugouts," she said.

"Hold on," I said as she went toward them.

"What?"

"Who do you think they belong to?" I asked.

"I don't see anyone," Kate said. "We could take one downstream."

"Steal a boat?" I asked.

"Sounds good to me," Max said, taking his time behind us.

"This is not good."

"Hey—I don't see any cliffs or walls or anything like that," Max called out. "As long as I don't see that and some devil's mouth, I'm fine."

We walked toward the edge of the river. We didn't see anybody along the shore.

"Finally we get lucky," Kate said.

But I didn't feel so lucky. The sandbank was narrow and shaped in a half-moon, with the open field of tall grass surrounding it, the dense jungle further in the background. Three dugouts were pulled up at the edge of the water.

"Let's get in one of these fast," Kate said.

"Just make sure no one follows us out of the jungle, okay?" I said to Max.

There was no reply.

I turned around.

He was gone.

This was confirmation that we weren't alone.

For a second I froze, facing the two-foot-tall grass and the jungle of hundred-year-old trees behind it. I could hear nothing and see nothing.

Max couldn't have simply disappeared. A lot had happened on this trip, but Max couldn't do a vanishing act.

I turned back to Kate.

"Get in one of those," I told her, pointing at the closest dugout.

"Where's Max?"

"Just get in!"

I raised my shotgun toward the surrounding, towering trees. A slight wind made the grass and trees wave back and forth. I held my breath, trying to listen, trying to still my heartbeat.

Something on my left . . .

I turned, the shotgun barrel following. Something in the grass shuffled.

"Max?" I shouted. "Max, you there?"

And then I heard something. Muffled.

My head spun around. Kate was guiding one of the dugouts into the water and looking back at me with hesitation. The forest we had walked out of looked darker, shadowed, sinister.

Something in the grass ahead of me moved.

Then I saw it. The dark skin, arms and shoulders, a figure running toward me, something in his hand.

I didn't wait to see what. The shotgun roared, and I felt the kick. The Indian was thrown back and crumpled into a grassy coffin.

"Hen—!"

Max was trying to call out my name. I cocked the shotgun again and waited.

Suddenly I saw his head rise up out of the tall grass. A dark hand was clamped over his mouth and an arm wrapped around his neck.

Then I saw another Indian next to him. Then another.

And then I saw more coming out of the trees. Two, four, seven, a dozen.

I turned around and saw Kate climbing into the dugout.

"Start paddling!"

The moment was surreal. I was going to die. Max and I were going to die in this uncharted spot in the middle of nowhere.

Max stared at me with a look that said *Just get out of here, you idiot! Go!*

The Indians started coming toward me, forming a half circle around me. Some carried primitive weapons, one carried a rock, another a long thing that resembled a spear.

"Max—" I started to say.

He nodded.

My eyes scanned all the Indians, then I turned and bolted toward the river. My legs didn't stop when they hit the water. I feared arrows flying at me, but for some reason none came.

I climbed into the wobbly dugout and grabbed the paddle Kate extended.

"Look," she said as I tried to move the canoe far from the shore.

Along the edge of the water, fifty—maybe more—naked, dark-skinned natives lined up to watch us glide away. None of them seemed to mind that we were slipping away, heading downstream.

Two of them held Max. He watched us as we moved further and further away.

"What are we going to do?"

All I wanted to do was get out of there. I couldn't think properly.

There needed to be some sort of plan, but I had nothing. Nothing at all.

"Henry?"

"I'm thinking. Or trying to."

"We can't leave Max there."

"Yes, we can. We just did. Not sure if you saw the fifty-something Indians standing there."

"Maybe we can talk to them."

"I just killed one of them."

Kate looked back, tears in her eyes. "But what—"

"Max will be fine."

"But what are we going to do?"

I shrugged. I didn't know. I couldn't shake the nagging dread filling me.

"What is it?" Kate asked, seeming to read my thoughts, or at least my face and body language.

"Do you get the feeling—does it seem like they *wanted* us to get in this dugout, to get us on this river?"

"They took Max."

"Yeah, but they could have stopped us from taking this. Or at least followed us. There were other dugouts they could have gotten in—and I'm guessing they're more skilled at paddling them than we are."

"What are you saying?" Kate asked.

"I'm saying that for some reason they wanted us to get on this river."

"If they wanted us dead, why didn't they just attack us?"

I nodded. "That's what I don't get."

"Should we stop?"

"No."

I pointed to the mountains ahead of us, their peaks jutting out beyond the treetops.

"We're heading toward that."

"What do you think is there?"

"That's where the map ends, right?"

"At least the portion I have."

"We're going to see what's down there. And then we're going to figure out a way to find Max."

"What if we don't?"

"We will," I told her. "Trust me, we'll see him again. We've gone through this before. He'll be fine."

"But will we?"

As if to answer her question, the daily rain arrived and poured down on us.

I looked at Kate, paddled on through the clear water, and smiled.

ON THE UNNAMED RIVER

February 6, 1929

After being soaked by the torrential downpour, we were quickly dried by the midday sun. The river headed ominously deep into the mountains, yet I could almost lose myself in the tranquility of the moment. The reflective surface of the water. Kate's long hair and bare arms and profile mirrored on the river as we glided down it. The soft sound of the paddles stroking the water. The symphony of wildlife, which either ignored our intrusion or didn't mind.

Why hadn't I met this woman somewhere else? And why couldn't I enjoy this moment instead of worrying about Max's life, not to mention our own?

It was an impossible question and one I didn't dwell on.

We coasted down the river in silence for a few moments. I considered our options, but none of them looked very good.

"See that?" Kate said suddenly.

"What?"

"Look at that. See that spider?"

I suddenly noticed what she was referring to. It was a spider the size of my hand, skipping across the surface of the river. It was colorful—predominantly orange—and it walked gently, floating on the river's crystal shell.

"That's unbelievable," she said.

"Too bad Max isn't here. He would know what kind of spider that is."

Kate turned around for a second, pushing her hair behind her shoulder. "What are we going to do?"

The peaceful interlude was over. Time to get down to business.

"I think those Indians might be from the lost city we're looking for. The map says we're close, right? We only have two more stages to go, according to that shaman."

"Stages?"

"You know what I mean," I said. "Whatever the seven signs are. We have two more to go. That means we're almost there."

"And then what?"

"If they had wanted to kill Max, they would have done so right away."

"Are you sure about that?"

I laughed. "I'm not sure of anything. I just saw a spider that can walk on water. All I know is that those Indians came from somewhere. They didn't make a trek a hundred miles—not a group that big. Their village must be close."

"But you said they wanted us on this river? Why?"

I shook my head. "I don't know. I just know that what we're looking for—your brother, this lost city, Max—I think it might be down this river."

"Beyond those mountains?"

"Maybe tucked inside of them."

"And if we find it? Then what?"

I scratched my beard. It was getting quite thick. "That's what I had Max for. We'd always figure it out as we went."

"Sorry I'm not of any help."

"Kate, please," I said with disbelief. "You've come this far, and I still haven't heard you complain."

"You've seen me cry."

"Not a big deal. You've got to let it out somehow."

"How do you let it out?" she asked.

"I store it up. And then I write it down. I purge myself through publication."

She chuckled and turned her head back to face the river in front of us, and continued to paddle.

So peaceful, that laugh. A man could almost lose himself in it.

The jungle surrounding us suddenly fell away and turned into steep cliffs. We found ourselves entering a canyon with sharp rock faces on either side of us. As we passed through, it felt as though we were being watched.

And warned.

"Do we keep going?" Kate asked.

"No sense turning around now."

"There's a *lot* of sense turning around now."

"No, there was a lot of sense turning around after we came upon the jaguar."

"Or the wild weeds."

"Sure. So what if this looks foreboding—if something happens and we can't escape to land? No problem."

Kate nodded. "Of course. No problem. Nice enough place to die."

We could see the crests of mountains in the distance. It had suddenly grown quiet, and the temperature had cooled.

The rock walls on either side of us were smooth, impossible to climb. I wondered how nature had carved them out.

"The walls of death," Kate said.

I nodded. "These appear to fit the description."

"Shouldn't there be something else, though? A wild octopus? Hail raining down from the sky? A leak in our dugout?"

"Give it time."

I could see Kate shiver.

"I hate this."

"What?"

"The unknown."

"We're going to be fine," I said. She didn't see my eyes dart to the shotgun that had suddenly become my closest ally.

"Hey—do you see that?" She pointed at the rock wall to one side. There seemed to be markings on it. We guided the canoe toward the edge of the stone so we could study them.

"They're carvings in the stone."

They were symbols, crudely etched but still obvious. One was of the sun, another the moon, one looked like some type of creature, another was of a man's head.

"Any idea what they might mean?" Kate asked.

"I'm thinking it means 'Don't trespass in the moody mountains, or else the sun and the moon will take off your head.' "

"I'm thinking it says 'All men from this point forward will be killed, women welcome.' "

"Yes, welcome to serve their meals and bake their breads and stir their pots."

"We'll be serving you up for dinner then."

The banter made us feel better about the unknown—at least I know it made me feel better.

We continued on, the cliffs surrounding us seeming to get taller the further down the river we went.

We would soon learn that there was truly no going back.

"Henry?"

"Yes, dear," I said as I took a slight break from paddling.

Kate had shifted in the dugout to face me. The boat drifted slightly downstream.

"So if we find this lost city, what then?"

"Well, I was thinking we'd rescue your brother, and then we might as well get Max while we're at it. Get some of that gold that's surely there."

"In a big pile," Kate said.

"Yes, in a big pile. Then find our way out. On the magical trail."

"Ah, yes, the magical trail."

I nodded. "And then of course we'll be heroes, and rich, and we can tell the world, and then last but certainly not least, I'll get the girl."

"Oh, you will, huh? And what girl might that be?"

"Well, there's only been one in this particular story."

"Ah, so of course, the hero naturally has to win the girl, correct?"

"Naturally," I said.

"I think the hero of this story might *be* the girl. What about that?"

"Then she deserves to win the heart of someone, right?"

"I call it more like a door prize."

"Ouch," I said, laughing.

My laugh was cut off in mid-guffaw.

Kate looked at me. "I don't think I want to know," she said.

"No, you don't. So I won't say anything about the half dozen Indians standing on the edge of the cliff."

Kate swung around and saw what I saw. At the top of the ledge on our left side, we could see a bunch of men, bows and spears in their hands.

They only stood, watching us, waiting. Waiting for something.

Our boat glided by underneath them.

"What do you think they want?"

I shook my head. "I don't know."

"Do you recognize any of them?"

"Well, they're wearing the same clothing as the ones who took Max."

"Stop—I'm serious."

"I can barely see them from here."

On the cliff to our right, another group of Indians stepped out next to the ledge. They also held weapons in their hands.

"They're letting us pass," Kate said.

I looked ahead down the river. It looked cloudy in the distance.

"They're letting us pass. But pass into what?"

Kate shot a glance back at me. Her body looked stiff, her face nervous.

"So what does the hero want to do now?" I asked her, trying to keep the mood light.

"The hero wants to be home in a nice hot bath listening to jazz."

"So we keep moving ahead."

The Indians above us—now actually behind us—just remained there, as if guarding something.

I had said we were close to something, and I was right.

We had arrived at the place we had been searching for.

There was one last hurdle to get over.

One very large hurdle.

We were about to discover the Devil's Mouth.

THE DEVIL'S MOUTH

February 6, 1929

The river cut through the canyon several hundred yards, then opened up as the walls fell away to a wider river mouth. We could see dozens of Indians standing on the top of the mountains, their weapons in hand, their bodies upright and on guard. The water pulled us forward more quickly as we entered the tranquil pool surrounded on all sides by hills.

Ahead was a cloud of mist. Unending, thick, breathing mist.

And then we could hear it.

Heavy, pulsating, violent, endless.

The sound of water gushing aggressively.

The unmistakable sound of water, falling.

"Henry?"

I nodded, my heart pounding, the boat continuing to move forward.

We were a hundred yards away from the mist, maybe more, but we could hear it and feel it, and we knew.

I put my paddle into the water to slow the boat from moving forward. It took all my strength.

"Henry?" Kate said again.

I need to let you know that I've been in other dire circumstances and outlandish situations where I felt the end had arrived. But I had never felt such dread and fear as I did sitting on that boat, the plume of vapor ahead of us, the booming noise of the falls surrounding us, and the Indians guarding the route behind us.

The walls of death.

That's why they were called that. Once you go through . . .

"Henry?" Kate said for the third time.

"Okay, we're going to be okay."

"What—do you hear—?"

"Yeah, yeah. Let's start paddling. Get your paddle."

For a second, all I could see were her shoulders bunched, her hands curled up tight.

"Kate? Kate, look at me. Look at me."

She turned. Her face was pale, her eyes vacant.

I grabbed her hand. The boat continued forward.

"Listen to me," I told her. "We're going to be okay. Just do as I say."

She nodded, tears rushing down her face.

"Paddle—come on, paddle with me. Let's get back out of here."

We pushed our paddles into the water and managed to get the boat back out, heading toward the canyon walls.

I could see more Indians on the ledges, and even more on the surrounding edges of the water where the canyon opened up.

As we approached the entrance to the canyon, a sudden flurry of sound and sight scattered across the water.

Dozens of streaking flames dropped before us, diving into the water. I looked up and could see more coming down.

They were arrows that were on fire, being sent down to the river between the rocky walls.

Kate covered her head. But I knew she didn't need to worry.

"Those are warnings," I said.

"Warnings? Warnings for what?"

"They don't want us turning back."

"Then what—what do they want?"

I looked back at the cloud of water behind us. Somewhere, the river dropped off into something, into some unseen and unknown bottom. I didn't know and didn't want to know.

But as the flaming arrows ripped through the surface of the water, I understood they would equally be content slicing through our flesh.

On each side of the river I could see forty or fifty Indians.

"They don't want us going back, I know that."

I could hear Kate weeping. I nudged ahead in the dugout and put a hand on her shoulder. As I did, the boat had its own mind and continued sliding along toward the noise.

Kate shivered. I held both of her arms tight.

"It's going to be okay."

She spoke in between her sobs. "This is my fault. We're all going to end up dead, and there was no—"

"Kate. Kate, look at me. Listen to me."

"What?"

"Don't do this."

"Don't do what?"

"Don't lose control. If it's going to happen, so be it."

She looked at me with an expression that said *Are you kidding me?* "What's that mean?"

"That means if you're going to die, you might as well have a smile on your face."

"That's the dumbest thing I've ever heard," she said, her face angry now.

I'd rather see her feisty than fearful.

"You want them to have the satisfaction of seeing you cry?"

"I don't care what they think. We need to go back."

"Why?" I asked.

She grabbed her paddle and starting violently working the water.

"Kate, stop."

"No!" she said, suddenly delirious.

We were in the middle of the opening where the river broadened.

"Stop, Kate. It's pointless."

"No, it's not!"

"What do you want? Do you want an arrow in your head? One in your shoulder blade? Possibly one in your back? Your knee?"

"Stop it!"

"If we go back they will kill us."

"We're going to die anyway."

I gripped the base of the paddle and held it firm. She tried to take it from me, but couldn't.

"You're right, Kate. We're going to die. We're all going to die, and maybe we die today and maybe tomorrow or maybe just maybe we'll die fifty years from now with thirty grandchildren and you'll be glad you listened to me because you went on living instead of doing something stupid."

"Do you hear that?"

"No, I'm deaf," I said.

"We can't survive that."

"You don't know that."

"Why—I don't understand. What do they want—why?"

"This is another culture and another land, and we're intruders. Maybe it's some sacrifice to the water god or sun god or god of frogs. I don't know. I don't care. I just know that I don't want to swallow an arrow that happens to be on fire, and I know I don't want to see you cut down by one."

She breathed in and composed herself, looking back at the Indians and then ahead of us. She wiped her damp, sweaty hair from her forehead and cheeks.

"Henry?"

"It's okay," I said to her, straddling her in the dugout the way a father might hold his daughter.

"It's not going to be okay. Don't lie to me."

"Yeah, okay. By the sound of those falls, it pretty much sounds like that's about the biggest waterfall we'll ever see in our lifetime."

"I've been to Niagara," Kate said.

"Yeah, me too. This sounds louder."

"Is that supposed to be comforting?"

I laughed. "Do you want comfort or do you want honesty?"

"I don't know what I want."

I could hear the sound of the falls in front of us all the way to my soul. It was deep, massive, raging. Like the entire earth was shaking from its core.

"Kate?" I said loudly, in her ear.

"What?"

"If you've ever had faith, now is the time to use it."

"'Use' it?"

"Pray. Do whatever it is you do."

Kate's body tightened up, shivering.

"I'm sorry," she said.

"For what?"

"For dragging you—for dragging everyone—into this."

"Kate?"

She arched her head again, her eyes locked onto mine.

I continued. "If I had to die with somebody, I'm glad it's you."

"I don't want to die. I know—I believe—I just—"

"I don't want to die either. I finally meet someone like you, and we're going over the waterfall."

"Literally," she said with a bitter laugh.

"Yes."

We had entered the mist and the dampness. It seemed like the water's edge must be close. It also seemed like the waterfall was wide and gaping.

Like an open mouth.

"This is where we end our search," I said.

"What do you mean?"

"I mean—this is it. This is the Devil's Mouth. I just hope we're not swallowed up by him."

The boat moved faster, the sound beat down on us, the sky absent, the water rushing everywhere.

And then we could see it.

The edge.

It looked like a million gallons of water were rushing over the edge of nothing.

We could see treetops far below.

How could we be this high up?

I could feel it coming, and my skin and my heart and my mind all raced *beating beating beating.*

I held Kate in my arms. I looked down at her, and her eyes were closed, her teeth clenched.

I remember thinking, hoping, that she was praying.

I didn't believe in God and didn't feel the need to pray. I wasn't scared to die. But I was scared that if I did live, Kate might not.

I yelled at her over the roar of the falls. "Whatever we fall into—fight, okay, Kate? Fight. Keep swimming—don't give up. We'll get out of this."

"Henry—"

We were so close. I looked down and saw that she had opened her eyes.

The falls were shaped in a smile, a half circle that seemed to suck in water viciously, violently.

I could see life and the sun and the jungle in the far distance.

I held Kate for what might be the last time, and I knew that I meant what I said.

If I had to die, I was glad to be dying at her side.

A man like me could spend his whole life searching and never find the one.

Our dugout was sucked in over the falls, and we were sucked in with it.

Falling in darkness.

Dropping into certain death.

But I didn't let go of Kate.

And I didn't close my eyes.

DARKNESS

February 6, 1929

Life doesn't rush in front of your eyes before you die. Instead, it gets silent and dark. And it feels like you can't breathe.

Or maybe that's just what happens when you go over massive falls that pour into white eternity, when you suddenly drop and wait for what's next.

I don't know if I almost died. All I know is that for a very long time, I was in silence and darkness.

But a very long time was probably a matter of mere seconds.

After that, I sucked in water and realized that I was still alive.

But very much in danger of dying.

It all happened so fast.

I found myself floating. I tried to move my arms, but I was toppling, turning. I couldn't see anything and I kept flipping, twirling.

I reached out to see if there was something to touch, but found nothing.

And all I knew to do was beat down with open palms and flail with my legs and feet.

Trying to get balance, trying to get control, trying to get out.

I needed to stop flailing around.

And somehow, in some way, amidst the burning in my stomach and the pounding in my head, I managed to get control.

And move.

So I moved upward, pushing, stroking.

And finally my head reached the surface.

And the sweet, glorious gush of air filled my lungs.

For a few moments, I couldn't make out anything. My head hurt too much, and I saw lights splintered across the sky as I breathed in and out.

Don't black out now, I told myself.

I saw a bright glow in the sky.

A rainbow.

Circling over the falls.

I floated in the cool lake a stone's throw from where the water fell. All around me, the jungle appeared wild, overgrown, undiscovered. There wasn't as much mist down here, but it still sounded loud. For a few minutes I just waded, my head hurting, my mind trying to take in what just happened.

I had survived.

But that was singular. There was no *we*.

I scanned the water's surface, calling out Kate's name. I tried to find the boat, but couldn't see anything.

I swam toward the cascading waters. I couldn't go under them—the force would send me deep underwater. But I waded toward their misty edge, still being hit and splashed, trying to find Kate.

This went on for several moments. Five, ten minutes.

I panicked.

Calling "Kate?" did nothing, even though I screamed it out.

I dived under the water and looked everywhere.

I couldn't see her blondish brown locks floating anywhere. Her creamy skin. Those long limbs and piercing eyes.

They were gone.

She was gone.

"Kate?" I screamed out.

Diving, wading, paddling, swimming . . .

Ten minutes turned into half an hour.

Nothing.

I had survived everything so far, including a rush over a two-hundred-and-fifty-foot waterfall, and I was alone.

I could deal with being alone.

I couldn't deal with losing Kate.

"Kate?" I cried out one last time, my tears blending into the fresh water from the river above.

From the middle of the large pool, a beautifully blue lake, the white foam of the water spilling out over it, the strokes of the rainbow smiling above, I looked at the sky.

My beliefs had proven true.

God was not there. He never had been and never would be.

We were alone from start to finish. And poor fools like Kate came and went believing in this nonsense, thinking it would help them. But even in those last seconds, it hadn't. Prayers weren't answered. Hopes weren't sustained.

In the end, all we had were ourselves and each other.

In the end, the notion of God was as foolish as trying to find some lost city in the jungle.

And just as I thought this, a sound made me turn my head.

In the distance, along the shore of the lake, I could see a figure.

Beautiful fiery, faith-filled Kate.

So her prayers had been answered.

I wondered if I'd been included in them.

I dived underwater and began swimming toward her.

But my happiness was short-lived.

Isn't it always?

He was unlike any Indian I'd ever seen. If that's indeed what he was.

He wore a headpiece. An ornate headpiece that was white and

shaped with snakelike curls. His body was painted with dark colors and exotic patterns. And he was huge. The biggest man I'd ever seen. He grabbed Kate by the arm and pulled at her, lifting her soaked figure off the ground, shoving her ahead. He didn't carry a weapon, but the other Indians—I counted four, five, six of them—did.

This stopped me from going further.

And then I saw something that nearly stopped my heart.

I saw Istu among the Indians. Not only was he there, but he seemed to be guiding the others along, talking to the big Indian and giving orders.

The men were standing at the opening in the jungle where the lake stopped. Because of the mist surrounding me, they had not yet seen me.

I quickly swam back, ducking under the water and going deep. I could hear the rushing falls above me as I swam beneath them, trying to get to the other side where I would be hidden behind the falling water.

For a brief second I thought of that Chicago night, diving into the river and out of harm's way.

Was this my lot in life? To be searching for the next big pool of water to dive into?

My lungs were almost ready to burst when I popped my head out of the water, sucking in the air, taking in my surroundings. The pouring water in front of me shielded me from the men. I saw the mountain behind me, the rocky and wet terrain.

Then I noticed something else.

The entrance to a cave.

But I needed to keep my eyes on Kate. I swam to the very edge of the curtain of water, where the flow wasn't as heavy. I could barely make out the figures in the distance.

The group was walking away, several Indians still poking about in the vegetation growing near the lake. Were they searching for me?

I wondered how Kate had managed to make it so far away from the falls.

She's strong, I thought. She's stronger than any of us on this expedition.

Another voice reminded me of what I had told her. *Fight, okay?*

The girl had a lot of fight in her, that was for sure.

As they led her away, into the jungle and whatever lay within, I hoped that Kate had a little more fight left in her.

She was going to need it.

Then I thought of Istu.

He had better have a little fight left in him, too. Because I knew I was going to kill him.

THE LOST CITY

February 6, 1929

I watched them. Their fires burned bright.

It was nighttime, and the jungle swayed with shadows. I hid on the edge of the village, watching the movement and life in silence.

So was this the lost city spoken about, dreamed about? It didn't glow in gold. Nor had I seen any strange and bizarre tribesmen. But they were certainly cut off from the rest of civilization.

I could still hear the faint sound of the falls in the background. Tall hills surrounded them on all other sides. These people were lost because they didn't want to be found.

I had crawled out of the lake and made my way in the direction Istu and the Indians had taken Kate. I had nothing left in my possession except the clothes I wore. Even my hat had been swept away by the falls. I didn't want to think of the obvious—the question of what would happen if we actually managed to escape. We wouldn't last long without weapons or food.

The village was next to the lake, in a clearing in the trees. Small huts were scattered around, several fire pits amidst them. Everything I saw looked ordinary, rather than ominous. Women walked with their children. Animals roamed the cleared land. Nothing seemed unusual except for the back of the village where a hill rose up. Beyond the huts, I could make out the top of what looked like a cross.

Perhaps it had been built by missionaries. Perhaps this was a peaceful tribe.

Maybe I could bargain with them.

Not that I had anything to bargain with. All this way, and I didn't even have a knife or a toy to exchange for food.

As evening settled in and the sun disappeared over the distant mountains, I smelled the dinner cooking over their fires and ignored my rumbling stomach. I couldn't see Kate or anyone else from my hiding place in the bushes.

When you're lying on your side tucked behind a tree, your head resting on your arms for support, the darkness covering you like a spiderweb, it's easy to fall asleep. The whole escaping from Indians with flaming arrows only to go over the dangerous falls thing helped too. And that's what happened to me. Sleep came quickly.

I awoke sometime in the middle of the night. It was strangely silent. Deathly silent.

Yet I could hear echoes of sound. I almost thought I could *feel* the sound, like a rumbling, coming from . . . beneath me?

I peered out from my hiding place. The village looked empty, the huts lifeless, the fires no longer aglow.

Something wasn't right.

I kept hearing (or was it feeling?) the beat of drums.

Without a soul in sight, I decided to take a look and find out where the noise was coming from.

The main beat I felt and heard was that of my own heart. Every step I made seemed louder than usual, every crack of a branch underneath my foot a potential giveaway.

I passed one of the cold fire pits and several huts, but nothing or no one could be seen. And with each step I took, the thumping grew louder.

At the back of the village stood an open area with a large cross in the middle. It was massive, consisting of two large tree trunks tied together somehow. It towered over me.

Behind it was a path that led toward the mountain. I followed it and from a distance saw the glowing mouth of a cave.

The pounding drumbeat sounded louder.

I thought of Kate and then thought of the shrunken heads, the shaman, the Indians who attacked us. And especially Istu.

Who knew what was going on inside that cave?

I would have felt much better carrying a shotgun.

As I drew closer I heard the sounds of people coming. I stepped off the path and hid in the brush in darkness.

Several men walked out of the cave, speaking in serious tones, their manner focused.

I let them pass and waited, still.

The drums continued.

I needed to get inside.

I sprinted toward the flickering light illuminating the opening of the cave.

My legs were sore, and I was tired and my belly was empty and my head still hurt from dropping down the falls, but I ran as though I was ten years younger. It's amazing what desperation can do.

Desperation. And fear.

There was a carved-out opening on either side of the cave with a fire burning inside. I wasn't sure how the flame was kept so intense and bright, but I didn't want to wait and find out. The entrance was large, but quickly narrowed to a small path. If it grew any narrower it would be suffocating; I could reach out and touch the wall on each side. I walked along it as the light from the entry grew more and more faint.

The passageway turned right in a ninety-degree angle, then proceeded to get larger. I could see more flickering, dim lights ahead. I was walking downward at a slow, steady pace. At one point the wall itself seemed to be moving. I studied it closer to see water trickling down it.

Another set of burning holes illuminated the narrow passage. The walls on both sides of me were painted in black symbols and drawings. I could make out a picture that resembled the waterfall.

Another seemed to be a set of crosses. Three of them. And what looked like skulls lying at their base.

I wondered what had created the tunnel I walked through. Surely it had not been the work of the Indians.

It narrowed then, and dropped at the same time, and a set of rudimentary stairs cut into the rock led downward. The light faded away, making me careful with each step I took. I could touch the ceiling above me and again could reach both walls. I just couldn't see down to where these stairs ended.

If anyone came up from below, I'd be in trouble.

Suddenly I was at the bottom—I nearly twisted my ankle, thinking there was another step. The temperature felt warm, the air stale.

Twenty or third yards ahead of me, I could see a round opening with light beyond.

I walked toward it.

When I reached the opening, I stood there, amazed.

My heart raced and my head felt light, and I tried to breathe in enough air.

This was the lost city spoken about in whispers, carried around in secretive rumors, dreamt about by fabled explorers and adventurers.

I had found it.

And there was no one with whom to share my excitement—and awe.

Somehow the entire belly of the mountain had been carved out. In its place was a city. Not a set of huts surrounding a campfire, not a string of rough lean-tos slapped together, but a city carved into the very core of this mountain cave. Hundreds of torches set along the walls and fastened into the stone dwellings lit the cave with a ghostly orange luminance.

The first thing my eye was drawn to was a massive pyramid in the center of the cavern. To give you an idea of how wide and open this cave was, the pyramid itself was probably twenty stories tall. The years it must have taken to build such a thing . . . and to build it in this place . . .

The thought took my breath away. What little breath I had.

As my gaze reached the top of the pyramid, another strong shape stood out in the dim light of the city. It seemed alien in this setting, and once again I wondered: *What is a cross doing here?*

It loomed over the pyramid and the city at its highest point.

A rustling sound made me turn around. I couldn't see anything in the darkness, but I knew I had to hide. I darted toward a large, life-sized stone carving of some strangely bored god that held its hands out.

The hands seemed to say *Go back home, you foolish, foolish man.*

The statue was big enough to hide me in the muted light.

Two Indians passed by, moving quietly. They wore headgear and were adorned with more clothing than the ones we'd seen along the river.

For some time the beating drums had ceased, but suddenly I heard them again.

I stood back up from behind the stone monument and studied the city again.

There were what looked like small dwelling places, huts of stone, built into the stone of the mountain. They were organized in a pattern around the pyramid. A dozen people, maybe more, walked around.

Even though it was nighttime, probably even after midnight, the city was awake.

The drums continued, and I slipped down a stone path, walking past a small pool of water. More strange sculptures adorned the path I walked along. Several were the shape of cats with wide mouths and fangs.

I could see fires at the top of the pyramid. I found another hiding place, behind some statues deep in shadow, and looked up to see what was happening.

Two Indians carried torches burning with fire. They stood on each side of the cross. I wondered if the pyramid was some sort of temple.

Then I saw another group of men approach the top. Istu was among them, carrying a long spear.

I soon saw another figure I recognized. One I knew too well, with a pale, narrow face and gray hair. Max stood in the center of the group, his hands tied in front of him, his face bloodied and worn.

And suddenly the beating of the drums and the lit fires and the towering cross all made me feel uneasy.

Very uneasy.

I wondered where Kate was.

INSIDE THE LOST CITY

February 7, 1929

A man painted in blood red proceeded up the stairs of the pyramid.

Crouched in my hiding place, I had a clear view of the figures at the top. The drum beat in synchrony with the movements of the red man with the long spear, advancing toward them. A crowd had gathered at the base.

By the looks of it, they had performed this ritual before.

Max jerked and pushed one of his guards away, but three more came to hold him down. Istu said something to Max, which got a response that the Indian didn't like. He slammed Max's side with the end of his spear.

I wished once more for the shotgun. Or any type of gun. I could scare off the Indians and try and rescue him.

The red man held his spear over his head and began to chant. The mass of bodies at the bottom of the pyramid chanted the same word back. The pounding drumbeat continued. I watched, mesmerized, occasionally looking over my shoulder to make sure I wasn't seen. It wouldn't help either of us if I joined Max.

Istu disappeared somewhere on the other side of the pyramid. Then he came back, a large cat flanking each of his sides.

That's impossible, I said to myself.

Istu led not one, but two jaguars, each on a short leash. One cat sat back on two legs and struck out a paw toward one of Max's guards. The Indian screamed and cowered. Istu jerked the rope back, and miraculously the jaguar sat obediently.

This was crazy.

And as I continued watching the scene in front of me unfold, I remembered something.

Dr. Helton.

He and Istu had "gone hunting" in the jungle. The good doctor had been dismembered by a jaguar, which to everybody including the Colonel seemed unusual.

Had Istu been responsible?

Watching now, I knew that he had been involved. I wasn't sure exactly how, or exactly why, but the Indian had been plotting against us the whole trip.

I looked at Max and wondered what he was thinking. He was probably wondering if he was going to be breakfast to the pet cats or just a toy for them to play with.

Again the red man and the crowd called back and forth in a series of chants.

And when the noise of the crowd died down, I heard another voice, high and angry and unmistakable.

Kate.

Kate was somewhere in this city, somewhere in this maze of stone structures.

She sounded furious.

I would find her, as soon as I rescued Max. One thing at a time. I didn't want to mess up and find myself the next item on the kitties' menu.

The chanting resumed. At one point the more aggressive jaguar jumped out again, this time toward Max. Istu surprisingly held it back, his strength obvious in the way he subdued this wild creature. The red man seemed unfazed by the jaguars, walking by them without any hesitation.

Another Indian appeared, the one I had seen earlier, wearing the white headpiece that looked like a skull. Strings of beads cascaded out of his ears and nose, and he carried a long sword.

Skull man waved the sword around, then approached Max, who stood with his arms locked by two Indians. In a grand gesture, skull man swung his weapon toward Max, then stepped away.

Max's side bled. The crowd went wild.

This wasn't happening. I wanted to rush the pyramid and take Max.

Be smart, a voice said to me. *Be smart. Don't do anything rash, or it will all be over.*

I couldn't just watch Max die up there. I wouldn't.

But they didn't intend to kill him quickly. While the red man chanted and Istu paraded the jaguars around, I saw two others lowering the cross.

Max was struggling, and I saw three men force him down. Then I realized what they were going to do.

They were tying him up on the cross.

It wasn't right.

All this way for this sort of end. This sort of death.

In the background, I could hear Kate's angry scream.

I sprinted down a narrow walkway toward her voice.

A hundred voices offered ideas on what to do, but I held them at bay while I went to find Kate and rescue her.

Then I would figure out how to do the same for Max.

If I had to kill a hundred of these crazy Indians, so be it. I would do it.

I simply needed to find a weapon.

As I made my way through the shadows, doing my best to stay out of sight, I thought about Max. About our friendship. How we had been in situations before where we thought it was over, and how we always managed to get away.

The voices kept chanting. The drums kept droning on.

I looked up at the pyramid and saw them putting the cross back upright. Max hung on it, his arms tied securely to the crosspiece.

At least they didn't nail him to it.

Every time things looked utterly bleak, it had been Max and I together, our heads on the chopping block, ready to die. And we always found a way out.

This time, it was all on my shoulders.

And I didn't have a clue what to do.

Kate would have an idea. Kate would be able to help. If, of course, I managed to find her. And get her free.

Thank goodness for her loud voice. It was getting louder.

Suddenly the beating of the drums stopped.

And the entire cave and city were immersed in something terrifying. Silence.

et us out of here now, you bunch of heathens! Get that man down! Get him down!"

The silence hadn't lasted long.

"You're not going to do that to him! You can't do that! Take him down now!"

Her voice was coming from a small chamber that appeared to be barricaded by a large stone. I couldn't help but think it resembled a tomb. Why not? They had a cross. I couldn't see any guards, so her captors must have considered her prison secure—or her screaming had sent them packing.

I approached the stone prison. There were a couple of gaps that allowed her to see outside.

"Somebody get me out of here! Get me out of here! You can't do this to me!"

I waited till she paused for breath. "Kate," I said in barely above a whisper.

"Take that man down! He doesn't deserve to be treated like that! Listen to me!"

"Boy, you have a set of lungs on you," I said in the next pause.

There was silence.

"Kate?"

"Henry?"

The openings in the stone were above our heads, so I couldn't see her. I kept looking around to make sure no one had spotted me.

"Henry, is that you?"

"Yes." I didn't hear anything for a minute. "Kate?"

"Yes. I just . . . I thought you had . . ."

"Yeah, well, I thought the same about you. Guess those prayers of yours worked."

"Do you see what they're doing to Max?"

"Yes. Are you hurt?"

"No."

"Listen—I'm going to get him. We're getting out of this place."

"How?"

"I have no idea. But I'll find a way. I'll get us out of here."

"Can you move the stone?"

The boulder in front of her tomb-chamber was as tall as I was. I leaned into it with all my strength, and it didn't budge. Not an inch.

"That thing's not going anywhere."

"What are you going to do?"

"Kate?"

"Yes."

"Have you—have you seen any signs of your brother?"

There was only silence, and silence could only mean one thing.

"No," she finally said.

I could tell she was crying, but trying to sound like she wasn't.

"If he's here, we'll find him. You just listen to me. You're going to be fine. We're going to be fine."

"Henry, I'm scared. Why are they doing this to Max?"

"I don't know. Maybe they got their religions confused or something."

"It was Istu who orchestrated all of this. He's been out to get us the entire time, he—"

"I know. I saw him."

"Who is that man in red?"

"I don't know. But I don't want to find out. I just want out of here."

"Henry, be careful."

"I will. Hey—we survived the waterfall. We can surely survive this."

"But what are you going to do?"

I looked up at the cross that seemed to float above us in the sky.

"I need to find a weapon."

"And then what?"

"Then just—I don't know. Kill about two hundred Indians. Take Max off the cross, move this boulder, and get you out of there. Try and find your brother. Then get out of here without being seen and escape through the jungle. No problem."

"Be careful, Henry," she said again.

"I will. Now don't go anywhere, okay?"

I heard what might have been a laugh. I hoped it was.

Footsteps. I held my breath and tried to slow down my heartbeat as I waited in the darkness of the hut, letting the men pass.

I was close to the pyramid, but had already avoided several groups of Indians. They were going back to what I assumed were their homes. But where did they actually live? In these dwellings of stone, or the huts outside the cave?

It smelled strange in the little building—like some unusual herb. There wasn't much inside the small dwelling, if that's what it was. Certainly nothing that looked like a weapon. I headed toward the open doorway—and froze.

Someone was coming in.

I tightened up, ready to attack or run if necessary. But as I did, I bumped into something behind me.

Whatever I touched fell to the ground.

The figure in the doorway turned toward me.

I could hear more voices outside.

I sprang toward the shadowy figure, wrapping both arms around it, my hands finding their way toward his throat.

The Indian wasn't big. Thankfully.

He writhed in my arms, but my hands gripped his throat and tightened around it.

The other men walked on by.

I squeezed. Harder. Harder. Harder. The man in my grip flailed his arms, his mouth uttering slight gasps, trying to call out, his legs moving but my legs staying put.

His body shuddered as I didn't let go, hoping he'd pass out.

I didn't know what else to do.

Fear and desperation make a person stronger. I knew this. I could feel it in my hands.

Soon the body grew limp, and I helped it slip to the ground.

I could see a little better now that my eyes were used to the darkness. I searched the room for something I could use as a weapon.
Perhaps a bow and arrow just sitting waiting to be used.

There was nothing.

I left the barely-breathing Indian on the floor of what was surely
his home.

I hoped they'd all go down that easily.

SECRETS OF THE CITY

February 7, 1929

İ turn my back for one minute, and look what you do."

Max opened his eyes and turned his head. "Couldn't you have gotten here just a little sooner? Before they decided to play Sunday school and put me on this ridiculous thing?"

"Are you okay?" I asked him as I crouched down, checking constantly in every direction to see if anyone was around.

"Sure, I'm fine. What do you think?"

"I mean—are you seriously hurt?"

"No, not at all. Can you see my face? Or my chest? I'm glad it finally stopped bleeding. I can't even feel my arms."

"I thought you'd be a little happier to see me."

"Where's Kate?"

"They have her locked up."

"Wow, you're doing well."

"You know, old man—we're lucky to be alive."

"Not me. I think my luck ran out after the crazy man with the fireballs."

I studied the cross. It was lodged into a hole in the pyramid's top, and by the looks of it the only way to move it would require men. And rope. Neither of which I had.

"You don't have a saw on you?"

I was glad Max could still joke. When the humor ran out, that's when I'd know things were dire.

Or more dire than this.

"Do you have any idea why they did this to you?"

"No. All I know is they're not interested in bartering. Or in anything other than sacrificing me."

"Did you see anybody else?"

Max looked down at me, gritting his teeth. He let out a groan.

"Yeah, but not who we're looking for. I got a glimpse of a woman —an older woman, white, probably scared out of her mind—in one of these underground rooms. There's a whole maze of tunnels in this place."

"Where were those rooms?"

Max told me how to find them. "But once you're in those tunnels, I have no idea how you'll get out."

"Any way out of this cave besides the main entrance?" I asked.

"How about you get me off this thing, and then I'll be able to think straight. Not to mention strangle of few of those Indians."

I looked around. "Look—I'll be back."

"Hey," Max said, "why don't I stay here and stake out the place? The view is pretty good."

"You know, I can't help but think of the irony of *you* hanging on this thing," I said.

"Just get me off of it. And soon."

"Yeah. Okay. I'll be back."

max was hanging on a cross. I wasn't sure if they were just going to leave him there to die, or if they had other plans.

Kate was stuck in a hollowed-out grotto with a giant boulder preventing her escape.

There was another woman who was surely being held here against her will. If she still had any will left.

And then there was Louis Prescott, who might or might not be stuck somewhere in another underground chamber. If he hadn't been hung on a cross himself.

The only thing standing in my way of rescuing these people was a tribe of about two hundred Indians. Including one really big guy with a helmet of bones and skulls and another guy doused with blood who liked to chant, and an Indian traitor who kept pet jaguars.

Then there was the labyrinth of tunnels and caves.

And the surrounding mountains and the waterfall.

And then the miles of jungle.

Things were looking bleak.

Maybe I should just join Max up there and get it over with.

I thought of this as I slipped down the stone stairs of the pyramid and back toward Kate's cell.

I needed a weapon. Something I could *do* something with. Cut rope or threaten an Indian or kill a wildcat.

You know—just in case.

I was lost.

I found the round opening in the rock that led to the series of tunnels Max described. Thankfully they were unguarded. I'd borrowed a burning torch on my way down the pyramid, and plunged into the pitch-black maze of tunnels to search for any sign of life.

The passages branched off so many times I had no idea what direction I was going, or whether I was going in circles. Every now and then I came across a room—a small, square hole that seemed to serve as a holding cell. In one I found a skeleton with a metal chain still attached to the leg, linking it to the stone wall.

I kept the torch at arm's length, the flames hot and stifling in this enclosed tube. Occasionally a lick of fire would lash out, burning some of the hairs on my arm.

I had been walking for an hour or more, or maybe only fifteen minutes, who could tell, when I heard a groaning call.

"Help."

I swung the torch toward the doorway and saw a woman crouching in a corner. Her long, gray matted hair covered most of her face. There was a blanket next to her, and on one side of the room was a bowl of water and another empty bowl.

"Help me, please," she said, in a voice so small I could hardly make out the words.

I placed the torch in a hole on the wall clearly meant to serve as a holder. The woman didn't move, and as I approached her I could smell a rank odor. I didn't know if it was just from the unclean conditions or if this was the smell of slow-moving but inevitable death.

I knelt next to her.

"Who are you?" she murmured.

"Who are *you*?" I replied.

"Ruth. Ruth Backary. My husband and I are missionaries."

"How long have you been here?" I asked as I propped her up to lean against me.

"I don't know. Years."

The thought was horrifying. But if I didn't want to end up like her, I knew I had to act quickly.

I got the bowl of water and held it to her lips. "Please, drink."

"Who are you?" she asked again.

"My name is Henry Wolfe. I'm on an expedition—to find a man named Louis Prescott."

"He's dead."

I looked at her. Surely my mouth was wide open and my eyes even wider.

This shouldn't have been a surprise. The only surprise would be getting out of this place alive.

But the goal of our trip was to find Louis. And if we were going to learn that he was dead, surely the news should come in a more dramatic way. Not casually, the way someone would say *It's Monday* or *I'm Sam.*

"How do you know?"

She took another sip from the water and coughed. "I'm sorry."

"No, no, it's fine. Look—I'm going to get you out of here."

"I can't go anywhere. I can barely walk. I wouldn't last a day in the jungle."

I breathed in and looked at her. "What happened to Louis Prescott? How do you know him?"

"They came after we had been here a year or two. Several months after Thomas was executed."

"I'm sorry," I said.

"The natives let us in. To live with them. To eat with them and sleep in their village. They showed us the city. But they believed they could have it—they thought they could do it themselves."

"I'm sorry . . . have what?"

"Eternal life. They believed they could have eternal life. And we told them they could—"

She coughed again, and I held her as her frail body shook.

"We told them the way. Christ's message of hope. But they twisted our words. They wanted to see it with their own eyes. So they made a cross and put Thomas on it, and they waited to see him die and then come back to life."

And they were trying again with Max.

"They understood the story. But they wanted to do it them-selves. They thought that if they killed the white man, then he would come back and bring with him eternal life. They even put Thomas in a tomb."

My mind reeled as all I could muster was an "I'm sorry."

"They did the same to the man named Prescott. Led him here

and then tortured him and put him on the cross."

"I don't get it."

"The man in red is their leader—he claims to have been living for over a thousand years."

"And has he? Is it true?"

The woman shook her head. There were deep lines in her dirty face, vacant eyes, a defeated frown.

"Of course not. I saw his father paint his own body and say the same things, and when he passed away, the son did the same thing. Yet they all act as though it's the same person. They're not a mean-spirited people; they are just ignorant. They want to *see* the hope we spoke about. They don't understand faith."

"So . . . did you see Louis Prescott die?"

The woman shook her head. I thought for a moment about Kate, about how I was going to tell her.

And Max. Max was still hanging on that cross.

"How did you get here?" Ruth asked me.

"It was a long journey."

"You can't go back through the front of the cave. They will soon know you're here."

"Is there another way out?"

She told me of the other exit while I tried to help her up.

"I can't go anywhere," she said.

"I'm not leaving you alone in this pitch-black cell."

"I'm not alone."

I looked at her. These weren't the words of a crazy woman.

"You don't have much time," she said. "It will be day soon. There is sunshine that lights this place during the day."

"What? How—"

"You'll see. You have to hurry."

"Please, Ruth, let me take you out of here."

"They don't hurt me."

"They've got you in a hole in the side of the mountain! They killed your husband."

"You have to leave while you can. If they see you, they will try to crucify you to bring you back to life."

My heart was racing, and my ears were hearing things, real or imagined I didn't know.

"Come on, let's get you to stand."

But she couldn't. Or wouldn't. Or both.

I felt like throwing her over my shoulder, but I couldn't carry her like that through the narrow passageways.

"Ruth, how can I leave you here?"

"You have others to rescue, don't you?"

"They crucified one of our party," I said.

She nodded, not surprised. "I know where they keep—things."

"What do you mean, *things*?"

"Things they've taken from outsiders. Things they don't know what to do with. Like—like guns."

I stared at her. "Where?"

"Go out of here and take three rights. You'll be at a dead end where you'll find a room. They don't know what to do with guns. But you probably do."

I nodded. Time was precious.

"Can I bring you anything?"

"I just want to see Thomas. He comes to me in my dreams. To

comfort me." She looked up at me and for the first time, she smiled.

"You don't believe me," she said. "Of course you don't."

"No, I—"

"It's okay. Are you a man of faith, Henry?"

"No," I said just as quickly as Ruth had said that Louis Prescott had died.

"All I know—the one thing I know after fifty-seven years of living—is that it's real. Maybe I was kept alive for a purpose."

"And what's that?"

She continued to smile, and reached for my hand. Her grip was surprisingly strong. "Maybe I was destined to meet you."

"I'm sorry that I can't—"

"It's okay. You need rescuing more than I do, Henry. You won't find the answers at the ends of the earth. The answers are right in front of you."

I nodded. Now I wanted to get out of here. I'd changed my mind about Ruth. The woman was batty.

"Henry, don't be like these Indians. So close to the truth and yet so far."

And with that I let go of her hand, took the torch, and walked away.

THE CAVES OF THE LOST CITY

February 7, 1929

I rounded the narrow corner and saw a tall figure fifteen feet away, holding a torch similar to mine. The Indian was as shocked to see me as I was to see him. The only difference was that I didn't hesitate.

I raced at him, torch in hand.

He barely could stand firm before I was upon him, the torch in his face.

The fire scorched his face as he screamed out and dropped back, stumbling across the floor. He dropped his torch, and I managed to stand over him, foot on his neck.

That's when I saw the other Indian.

This one was holding a knife. A knife that looked American made.

Perhaps it had belonged to Louis. Or the missionaries.

I didn't think long about this as I hurled the torch at his head. The Indian ducked, and as he did I raced toward him, my body low, my shoulder firm. I decked him like a football player making a clean tackle. He fell back, and I heard the clang of the knife on the ground.

The first Indian was behind me, torch in hand.

I found the knife and scooped it up in my hand.

Again, I wasn't thinking. I was reacting. Or rather, simply acting, playing the part of the hero as if I'd engaged in hand-to-hand combat before.

I rushed toward the first Indian, blade outstretched. He defended himself with the torch, swinging it wildly.

Behind me, the second Indian started toward me.

This could have been the end.

But I knelt to one side and let him pass. He was too big to be agile, and his massive body passed mine like a galloping bull missing its mark. As he tried to stop, I wrapped my left arm around his body and planted the knife in my right hand firmly into his back. He didn't howl as I expected; instead he stiffened.

The first Indian still rushed at us, but instead of engulfing me in flames, he burned his buddy. If they weren't trying to kill me, I might have felt bad. But I didn't.

I pulled the knife from the Indian's back and started to go for the first guy. He dropped his torch and sprinted off.

I thought of chasing him, but I knew he could outrun me and also lead me into danger.

If Ruth was correct, these Indians had been guarding a room full of items taken from visitors.

I recovered the torch and looked into the room.

I smiled.

I wouldn't need the knife anymore.

For another twenty or thirty minutes—time seemed to be a stranger to me—I walked through the tunnels. I never did pass Ruth again, even though I would have sworn a room I passed was hers. It took me forever to finally get out of the tunnels. And when I did, it seemed like morning had come.

Daylight shone in various places around the cave. The most obvious was the light shining down on Max. His body looked lifeless, unmoving on the wooden beams.

I knew I had to get him down.

And I was weighted down with items that would help me do just that.

But first I needed to get Kate.

The only problem was that when I reached her holding cell, the stone had been moved and she had been taken away.

Or resurrected, a voice told me.

Yeah, or that. One of the two. My hunch was that either way she was still with the Indians.

Maybe the one Indian had told his buddies about me.

I didn't want to wait to see others. I looked up at the pyramid looming over the village. I knew I needed to get Max and then search for Kate.

And then, if I found her, and if we escaped, somehow I'd manage to tell her about her brother.

All this way for this.

The only treasure I'd seen was a roomful of stolen artifacts and weapons.

So much for the glorious missing city.

Some things weren't meant to be found.

Sunlight beamed down on Max. I approached the pyramid, hiding behind rocks and dwellings and staying in the shadows until I reached the massive stone triangle. I went to the back side—there were two staircases that led to the top. Considering I hadn't eaten in a day (maybe two, I wasn't sure) and hadn't slept much, it was quite a task to ascend this thing again. Each step was about three feet tall.

I reached the top of the pyramid and didn't see anyone. Max was facing the other way. I knelt down and took off the three guns I had strapped over my shoulder.

I was breathing heavily. This was probably why I didn't hear the footsteps behind me until my assailant was upon me.

Just as something came crashing down toward me, I jumped away, barely escaping with my life.

My head would have been cracked like a watermelon.

The blunt instrument looked like a croquet stick, except made of stone and a lot denser. The square top crashed to the stone floor.

I turned around and saw the red man. Naked except for some type of strange feather dress, also red, belted around his waist. I tried to reach for a gun, but the stone mallet was poised to strike again.

I rolled on the stone surface, cutting my arm and face as I did.

The red man was now between me and my supply of weapons.

I reached for the pistol in my belt, but again the man in red swung the instrument. This time it struck my arm, nearly breaking it. The pain was intense, and the force knocked me to the ground.

I saw the stone hammer rise up for another blow.

I didn't have time to reach for my gun.

So I did the only other thing I knew to do. I kicked him, and kicked him hard, in his stomach.

He stopped and looked amused. It seemed to do nothing.

He brought the mallet down and again barely missed my chest as I rolled over.

I grabbed a knife I had taken and tried to grasp it, but the Indian was behind me, his arms locked against my neck, suffocating me. The knife fell to the ground, the place all my weapons seemed to end up.

I gave him an elbow in the gut, but again he barely reacted.

I was seeing stars.

I reached for air. Nothing.

Again I tried to jerk at him, tried to fend him off, tried for something.

Nothing.

"Max," I said as the world started to go black.

And then a loud boom sounded, and I felt air rush back into my lungs as the grip on my neck loosened when my attacker turned toward the blast. In that split second I was able to twist free and grab my gun. I fired at him without stopping to think.

I landed on my knees and keeled over, sucking in air and coughing. I turned around and saw Ruth standing at the base of the pyramid, shotgun in hand.

I tried to breathe again, tried to get rid of the dizzy feeling.

"I decided to follow you out," she said.

"Henry? That you? Who else is there?" Max called.

"I'm getting you down," I said.

"Did you bring reinforcements?"

Ruth walked around and stood with me at the base of the cross.

Max looked amused. "Always need someone to bail you out, don't you?"

"I might leave you up there if you keep that up," I said.

"Where's Kate?"

"I don't know," I said. "But we're going to find her and get out of here."

"Just one thing," Max said as I cut the cords around his legs first. "Whatever you do, don't do anything to that Indian in the red paint. He's like some god around here. If something happens to him, these Indians are going to be pretty incensed."

I looked at the crimson corpse sprawled out on the rocky surface. "Nothing's going to happen to him. Nothing at all."

INSIDE THE CAVES

"Hide in there!"

I helped Ruth into the empty hut, and Max followed. We hid behind anything we could find—a basket, a table—as we heard Indians passing. Their voices sounded angry, their footsteps determined. We'd been lucky to get down off the pyramid without being seen. But someone had heard the shotgun blast, and by now they had surely seen what that blast had done.

After the Indians were gone, I asked Ruth if she had any ideas where they might be holding Kate.

"Are there any other crosses lying around?" Max said, only partly in jest.

I shot him a glance that surely showed my anger.

"Henry, if we don't find her soon, we might have to—"

"Don't finish that thought," I told him abruptly. "Don't even begin to finish that thought."

"My thought is simply that we're running out of time."

"Kate wanted to find you, Max."

"And I want to find her."

"Good. Then we start looking. And we don't stop until we find her."

Max wanted to say something, I could see it in his face, but he remained silent.

"Is there any other special place in this city?" I asked Ruth. "Besides the pyramid?"

"There's the head of the jaguar."

"The what?" Max asked.

"It's an idol made of gold. They worship it. And baptize their children there."

"What kind of strange religion do these people have?" Max asked.

"Let's go there," I said.

"The only thing . . ."

I waited for Ruth to finish.

"There are live jaguars by the idol. To protect it."

"We've encountered jaguars before," I said. "And this time we've got guns."

There was a flat area of dirt, and in the center was a stone block six feet tall by six feet wide. And surrounding it, a loud crowd.

I could see Kate standing on top of the stone block next to the tall Indian in the skull helmet. Her hands were bound—I couldn't see her feet.

In the center of the block sat a small pyramid-shaped table holding what I assumed was the "head of the jaguar." It was gold and the size of a football.

I heard a high-pitched, blood-curdling scream and for a second thought it was Kate. Then I realized it was the cry of a jaguar.

A second roar sounded, again high and screeching.

The crowd applauded. The jaguars continued to shriek and scream.

Skull man took the gold idol and held it high above his head.

Kate looked terrified.

"Max?" I said softly.

He was right beside me and simply glanced my way.

"We have to move now," I said.

He nodded.

"You know the plan, right?"

He nodded again.

"Think we'll be okay?"

The ferocious wail of both jaguars sounded. The crowd continued to chant.

"Of course we will be," he said with a fake smile.

The crowd surrounded the stone platform. Max and I rushed toward them, shotguns in hand. I still couldn't see the jaguars, but that didn't matter.

The main thing was getting to Kate.

Max led and fired off a shot into the sky. The crowd turned, some of them fleeing, some of them acting like they might attack.

I fired off another shot as a warning, and the Indians started to disperse. As they did, the sea of bodies opening up, I could finally see the wild animals.

There were two of them, one tied on either side of the stone block, pawing and scratching the air and the ground and trying to get to one another.

An Indian rushed at me, and I batted his head with the butt of the shotgun.

Max walked ahead, the shotgun pointed at anyone in front of him. "Get away—go on. Shoo. Get out of here."

I ran toward the base of the stone platform, and one of the jaguars launched itself at me. The rope pulled it back, seizing its neck and sending it twisting to the ground.

"Henry!"

I knew Kate had seen me, but so had skullhead.

"Henry, watch out!"

I turned to my right to see who was there, then felt a blow to the left side of my head.

It felt like a rock.

I stumbled to the ground.

A shotgun blast roared. Then another. There was a cry, a scream, the roar of the jaguar, the sound of something falling in the dirt.

On my hands and knees, I tried to regain my vision.

The shotgun fired again.

I couldn't see where mine had gone.

"Henry, help me!"

I got back up on my feet and continued running toward the block, passing a few Indians who seemed more afraid than anything else.

The big Indian held Kate in one arm, a long sword in the other. The man's eyes were wide and wild.

I looked out at the crowd and saw Max wrestling three Indians. His shotgun was nowhere to be seen.

One jaguar was lying on the ground, while the other was jumping and clawing and trying to strike out at anything around it.

"What are you doing?" Kate screamed.

"What do you think we're doing? We're getting you out of here!"

She looked angry. Unbelievably angry. At me.

"You call this a rescue!"

The Indian tightened his hold on her and pointed the sword at me, waving it, a warning to get away.

"Did you find him?" she called out.

"Kate—"

"Henry, tell me."

"Kate, no—"

"Did you find Louis?"

She twisted and turned as the Indian held her.

I slowly pulled a .45 from my belt.

"Kate—he's not here to be found."

She looked at me then, and knew. For one second, she closed her eyes.

I started to raise my hand, when Kate suddenly kicked up her leg and dug her heel into the Indian's shin. Then she jerked both elbows back into his stomach, loosening his grip on her.

She managed to wiggle free of him for just a moment. He tried to regain his balance, but as he did, I fired off a shot.

It nearly hit Kate.

The second shot found its way to the Indian's thigh. He dropped the sword and howled in pain.

I fired another that hit his chest and sent him down for good.

"Take this," I told Kate as I gave her the gun.

There was no time to talk. No time for anything.

I took my knife out of its sheath and bent over the side of the platform. Quickly, frantically, I cut the rope binding the second jaguar to the edge of the block.

The jaguar roared to life and sprang on the closest person it could find. It was one of the Indians holding Max.

The poor guy never knew what bit him.

I'll never forget that sound, the sound of a caged wild animal finally getting free, finally able to attack his guardians, finally able to act out what had surely been in his imagination for a very long time.

Max managed to retrieve a shotgun and rushed to the stage.

"Took you long enough," I told him.

"That knot on your head looks pretty bad," he said.

I rolled my palm against the golf ball-sized knot on my forehead. "Could be worse."

Max hugged Kate. "Are you okay?"

"Are *you* okay?" she asked him.

"We need to get out of here."

Kate looked at me. I knew what she was thinking.

There is nothing left here. We came here to find Louis, but he isn't here.

"Yeah, let's go."

There would be more to say. If only we could get out of this place.

THE UNDERGROUND POOL

February 7, 1929

"They're coming."

"You need to go in first."

I looked at Max, then at Kate and Ruth.

"I need to go last," I said.

"And why's that?"

"In case some of our friends decide to join us."

I was thinking of one in particular. Istu had conveniently vanished as usual just when things were getting rough. But I was betting he would show up again.

I wanted to be there when he did.

We stood near a pool of water that edged the side of the cave. We had fended off the remaining Indians, but we knew they were coming back. Their two leaders had been killed.

Both by me.

Ruth said this was the only other way out. The entrance to the cave would surely be blocked by now.

"Okay, fine. If you guys aren't going to do it, as usual, I'll take the lead," Kate said.

"No, wait, I'll go first," Max said. "So tell me again—I just swim underneath this rock, straight ahead toward the light. Right?"

"Yes. That's what we heard, anyway. And I've seen Indians coming out of there. It can be done."

"What if there are Indians waiting on the other side?"

"That's why you're going first," I told Max.

"We need to hurry," Kate said.

Max stepped in the water and sank down to his neck. He carried a knife and a pistol.

"Well, if this is it, then *au revoir*."

He sucked in a deep breath, then dived into the water.

We waited to see if he would come back up, but he didn't.

"Ruth, why don't you go next?" Kate suggested.

"I'm not sure if I can."

"I'll help you."

"Kate, no, I will," I said. "You go first."

"No."

"Look, I wasn't the one imprisoned. I can hold my breath for a long time. I'll be okay. Let me help her."

"That's fine," Ruth said.

Kate looked at me, then looked out at the cave, a sad expression on her face.

This was our final destination. And we were leaving without the person we'd come all this way to find.

Kate slipped into the pool and waded to the edge of the rock, took a deep breath, and plunged underneath the surface.

That left two of us.

"Henry?"

I knew what Ruth was about to say.

I wasn't sure what I'd say in reply.

I'd already left her on her own once. And she had come back. I owed my life to this woman.

"Kate is Louis Prescott's sister, isn't she?"

"Yes."

"I recognized her the moment I saw her. They look a lot alike."

"She was the one who organized this expedition. Led it, actually. She's a tough girl."

"Her brother was tough, too. To the very end."

A group of Indians turned the corner and saw us. I fired a couple shots from my pistol to keep them away.

"We have to go, Ruth."

"I need to tell you something before we go. In case—"

"There's no need to do anything 'in case.' You're going to make it. I'm not leaving you behind."

"No, please, Henry, listen."

So I did. And Ruth told me her story, quickly and deliberately.

Then we both got into the water. I let her go first.

Imagine two ponds of water, connected by an underground tunnel big enough to swim through, but only wide enough for one person to go through at a time. Imagine this tunnel surrounded on all sides by tons of stone and rock. Imagine how dark a tunnel this would be, and how daunting a task it would be to swim through it.

If you were someone my age, it would be daunting enough.

But for Ruth, it was so much more.

And midway through swimming the tunnel, something happened.

I believe she panicked.

And it almost killed us both.

I was swimming with all my might when I ran into Ruth. My head hit her back.

I couldn't see a thing. Then I felt flailing arms.

I grabbed one and tried to hold it still. Then I tried to guide her along.

The arm pulled away.

I backed up and found her again.

My lungs were starting to burn.

I reached out and grabbed her shoulder, pulling it toward me.

Her hands pushed me away.

I swam down and reached for her legs to see if they might be stuck. But like her arms, they were thrashing around. At one point her knee connected with my nose.

I accidentally sucked in some water.

Angry now, my head pounding and my chest clawing for air, I grabbed on to her hand one more time.

I jerked it and tried to get her to go with me.

But she wouldn't.

I didn't see light, and knew I still had a long way to swim.

I didn't want to leave her.

But I wanted to live.

So I let her go and pumped my arms and legs as fast as I could down the narrow tunnel.

I felt lightheaded, terrified, rushed. My lungs craved air.

I kept swimming, paddling, kicking.

I'm not going to die like this, I thought in anger. *Not after everything else.*

My nose throbbed and my eyes started to see lights and I wondered if this was it, if I was going to pass out and die. . . .

But the lights I saw came from the pool of water just beyond.

A hundred feet or less.

So I raced toward it.

My heart and soul and lungs reeling.

Until I finally managed to slip through the hole on the side of the mountain and race to the surface of the lake.

I almost jumped out of the water.

I sucked in the sweet, glorious air and for a second couldn't see anything, couldn't do anything except breathe in.

Breathe in. And breathe out.

Took you long enough," Max said.

I could see his head floating on the lake's surface.

"Yeah, I was having second thoughts," I said. "I was having so much fun back in that cave."

"Where's Ruth?" Kate said.

"She didn't make it."

"Seriously?"

"Seriously."

"Is your nose bleeding?" Kate asked, swimming closer.

I could hear the sound of the waterfall in the distance.

"Yeah, Ruth's knee connected with my nose. I think she panicked back there."

"I panicked too," Kate said. "I thought I was going the wrong way."

She wiped my face with her hand and accidentally drifted into me. For a second, I could feel her warmth.

"Sorry, I was just trying—the blood—"

"Look, you two, there'll be time for that later," Max said. "We have to get out of here."

Kate looked shy for a second. For such a strong woman, she could also have the expression of a twelve-year-old girl.

"So she said we have to go *behind* the falls, right?"

"Yes," I said. "There are caves behind the falls. I saw them myself."

"How do we get to them?" Kate asked.

"Suck in as much air as we can, then dive down deep to avoid the current and undertow."

We looked at the massive water pouring down from the cliff above.

It was easier said than done.

"Give me just a minute," I said. "I need to catch my breath."

"I don't think we have time."

Max nodded toward the land where we could see a group of Indians coming.

"Okay," I said. "Time to go. Kate, you ready?"

She nodded at me. So much to talk about.

Especially now.

THE CAVES BEHIND THE FALLS

February 7, 1929

Did she give you any tips which direction to go?"

I couldn't see Max, but I knew he stood right next to me. We had gone from one dark, underground passage to another. Thankfully, this one wasn't full of water, even though we were still soaked.

"I'm not sure if Ruth even knew. All she said was that there was a way out of here through the caves behind the falls."

"There are two different ways to go," Max said.

I could hear him tapping the walls with a stick he had found when we entered the caves.

I was surprised at how easy it was to go under the falls the second time. I had dived deep and then swum behind the rushing water toward the small beach that led into an open cave behind it. We hadn't thought of the light issue—perhaps we were hoping there would be magically lit torches to guide us through. So far we had been stumbling through the darkness for half an hour.

"Kate, what do you think?"

"I don't know any more than either of you."

"Then take a guess. Which way do you want to go?"

For a moment there was just silence.

"Kate, you there?" Max asked.

I heard a sniffle.

I found her in the darkness and held her in my arms.

"We'll go right," I said to Max. "Just . . . in a few moments."

Kate cried, as silently as she could, in the darkness of the cave, the reality surely settling in. Her face was buried in my wet shirt, her hands digging into my back.

I held her tight, wanting her to know that I wasn't going anywhere and that things were going to be okay.

But I couldn't bring her brother back.

I didn't want to tell her what else Ruth had said. Not with Max within range.

She needed to know, but I knew she didn't want to talk now.

She needed to let it out.

So she did.

You guys are going too fast," Kate said.

"Here, take my hand."

"It's not like I'm going to get lost."

"Kate?"

"Okay, fine. It's fine. I'm fine. It's just—you're going so fast. I've almost tripped four times. I don't want to fall and land on the edge of a rock."

"Hey, Max?"

"I can hear you," our leader said. "I just want to get out of these caves. Remind me that I never in my life again want to go inside a cave. Any cave of any kind."

"That makes two of us," Kate said.

We had been in the darkness for at least two hours now. I was beginning to feel claustrophobic. That, combined with not knowing if we were going the right direction, made our moods hopeless and exasperated.

"This better lead to somewhere," Max said.

"Hey, Max," I said, desperate for lightness in every sense of the word. "This would be a good place in the story to have a wild beast in these caves."

"No, that wouldn't work," Kate said from behind me, still holding on to my hand.

"Why not?"

"Well, you don't want to repeat yourself. We had jaguars—on two different occasions—along with the piranha."

"I agree with Kate," Max said. "A wild animal would be redundant."

"Not to mention that it would probably kill all of us."

"No, what you need is a spirit," Kate said.

"A devil," Max agreed. "Obviously, since we're at the Devil's Mouth. Or underneath it now. Or beside it. Who knows where we're at. But a devil running around—now that would give your story an added touch."

"Are you going to write about this?" Kate asked.

"First I'd like to get back to America. And then, yes, maybe. Of course."

"Don't tell people they stuck me on a cross," Max said. "That's a bit strange, don't you think?"

"Those Indians had a truly warped version of Christianity."

"Maybe it was the missionaries' fault. Maybe they didn't do a good enough job explaining it."

"I doubt that," I told Max. "Ruth told me the Indians just took the parts they wanted. They wanted God to visit them, to give them eternal life right here and now."

"They were crazy. But good fodder for another story."

There was silence.

"Not that any of this was *good*," Max added, surely for Kate.

"You could add a ghost in here," Kate said. "It would be spooky, but perhaps it could light up the caverns and lead us out."

"Yeah, right straight over a cliff," Max said.

"This isn't a ghost story," I said.

"Sure it is," Kate said. "It has ghostly elements. I mean—explain those vines to me."

"Yeah, that was strange."

"Strange?" Max said. "A woman who keeps fifty cats is strange. Vines that come out of the jungle and try to kill you—that's more than strange."

"I'm sorry, Mr. Poet. What word would you like me to use?"

"Supernatural," Max said.

"See—it is a ghost story," Kate added.

The passage we were in was descending. "You don't think this is leading us back down underground?" I asked.

"Who knows," Max said.

"Trolls," Kate said with a laugh.

"What?" both Max and I asked.

"Trolls. That's what we need now. Cave trolls."

"For what?"

"To make the story complete," she said, squeezing my hand a couple of times. "We need a few trolls to chase us around these caves."

"Give us time," Max said. "We'll find them. God only knows what else we'll find."

"He actually does know what we'll find."

"That was a figure of speech," Max said.

"And it was an accurate one."

Max only laughed.

Is that light?"

I squinted my eyes and could see it. A small trace of light leaking over the wall.

"Max?" I asked.

"Yeah, it's light," he said. "There's something ahead."

"We should take bets on what it is," I said.

"What do you have to bet?" Max asked.

"I've been holding on to this candy bar for several weeks now," I said with a chuckle.

"I can't wait to get out of here and breathe fresh air," Kate said.

The cavern had leveled out, and we were walking straight now. The passageway turned a few corners, and we soon saw the opening.

"What if it leads us to the middle of the jungle?" Kate asked.

"We are in the middle of the jungle," Max replied.

"Yes, but what if—?"

Max reached the round entrance to the cave. "Well."

"'Well'?" Kate said behind me. "What's that mean?"

"It doesn't sound like a bad *well*," I told her.

"We're not dead yet," Max said, looking back at us. "And it seems like the gods—or God—shined down on us this time."

We reached the edge of the cave and saw what he was talking about.

Kate hugged me.

It wasn't salvation.

But it was something.

ON THE SHORE

We sat on a praia somewhere in the middle of Brazil along an unnamed river. Next to us sat a dugout, ready and waiting to be taken out. There was no question whether or not to steal it. The Indians had taken enough from us, and if we lingered any longer, they would take something else. We wanted to rest for a few minutes, let the sun shine down on our faces and arms and foreheads as we breathed in fresh air and quietly took stock.

The silence grew to a point where it seemed impossible to break, as though something bad might happen if someone spoke.

So, of course, I did.

"Where do you think this heads?" I asked.

They both gave me unsure and annoyed looks.

"It seems like it's heading north," I added.

Neither of them spoke.

I rubbed my temples and closed my eyes for a second. The sun was bright, and it was taking awhile to get used to being outside again.

"You guys think this rifle will work after being in the water?" I asked as I looked down at the gun drying in the sun.

"Only one way to find out," Max said.

"Thanks. That's helpful."

"That's why I'm here."

I stood up. I could understand Kate's mood and silence, but Max was an entirely different story. I assumed it was because we had come all this way and had come up with nothing. Nothing except a story about a lost city, the same thing everyone came back with, if they came back at all.

"I'm going to excuse myself for a moment, and then I think we should get going," I said, heading into the jungle behind us.

The sand turned into grass and dirt, and soon I found myself under a large tree. As I turned to head back to the dugout, I saw a face staring at me.

A dark face with no hair and a bone through the nose.

Unless Max had suddenly figured out a way to shave, get a tan, and pierce his nose, I was in trouble.

The figure lunged at me and seized my throat. The hands were long and lean, and tightened around my neck with a terrifying fury.

I fell back against a bush. For a second I lost my breath and my bearings with this Indian on top of me. I flailed my arms and legs as I tried to move out from underneath him. Thankfully he wasn't big, so I was able to push him off me. I did this by clawing at his ear, taking hold of it, and almost pulling it off.

As he howled and I got back up on my feet, I looked deeper into the jungle. There were four more men.

And then I saw him.

Istu had decided to make another appearance.

The Indian in front of me stood up, and just as he did I kicked him in the chest, sending him back against a tree. I quickly looked on the ground for any weapon he might have had, then stared at him.

He had nothing.

I turned and faced the approaching Indians. I caught one aiming his bow at me, and just as he let go I bolted to my right, barely missing the arrow. The nearest Indian was upon me now, this one carrying an axe of some kind. He flung it in a cumbersome and awkward way, as though he had no idea what to do with it. As his arm lofted it through the air, hitting nothing, I crushed my boot down on his ankle. The force and the angle did something right, because not only did I hear a *crack*, but the Indian yelped in pain.

He dropped the axe, and I knelt to pick it up, again avoiding an arrow that I heard land against a nearby tree.

"Max! We've got trouble!" I yelled as I turned and started running toward the shore.

The first Indian blocked my path. I didn't hesitate, but ran toward him with the axe. He stood, holding his arms up, not in a posture of attack but more in a frightened stance, looking at the weapon in my hand and hearing the other Indian screaming. He turned and ran for the shore.

"Max! Kate! Get the boat in the water!"

The stillness of the afternoon was quiet enough for my voice to echo. Surely they had heard me.

If not, the parade was coming. They'd see us soon enough.

The bewildered Indian running for his life.

The axe-wielding crazy writer who had spent a few too many days out in the wilderness.

And three Indians following, one who kept firing arrows and missing.

"Max! Get the guns!"

When the shore was in view, there was no one in sight.

No Max and Kate.

No dugout.

The Indian running away from me had nowhere to go as the river loomed, but that didn't matter when an unseen force knocked him over. His head jerked, and he dropped instantly.

The unseen force was a rifle shot. The bullet had hit the Indian in the head. I looked around quickly, but still couldn't see Max and Kate.

Behind me the Indians suddenly stopped in their tracks. Even the arrow-firing Indian stopped what he was doing.

Istu smiled and aimed a pistol at me. He fired three successive rounds.

Thankfully he was a bad shot.

I ducked and tasted sand as I crawled toward cover.

Several more shots were fired, coming from my right. I looked over and saw Kate firing the rifle from behind a patch of brush. Max was behind her, struggling with his pistol, which obviously wasn't working.

"Get the dugout on the river!" I yelled.

The dugout was next to them, and Max pushed it into the water as Kate fired off another round.

One of the Indians bolted back into the woods. Istu fired his gun, but then appeared to be out of bullets.

A round from Kate's rifle sent the Indian with the bow to his knees.

Standing again, I faced Istu. And then I did something very stupid.

I ran toward him, axe in hand.

I probably wouldn't have, except for the sneer on his face.

"Henry!"

Kate's voice didn't stop me.

He threw his pistol at me, but missed.

"You need to take some firing lessons," I said to him.

He pulled out a knife the size of my forearm and laughed. "I'm better with this."

The Indian next to him reached for another arrow. I was blocking Kate's view, so she couldn't fire.

Indian with a large knife plus Indian with a bow and arrow equals trouble.

The sun and the sand and the stress all came together at once, and I lunged toward Istu. The axe came crashing down on the knife and sent it flying out of his hands.

The other Indian watched us both go tumbling onto the ground.

As we did, another shot was fired.

I believe it might have hit me had I been a foot higher on the ground.

The Indian with the bow took off.

Now it was just Istu and me.

His knife was somewhere, I wasn't sure where. He grabbed my right hand. The strength of this man was unbelievable. Soon I dropped the axe. His other hand clawed at my neck, my throat, and squeezed.

I pawed at him with my right hand, pushing his cheek away, then slamming my fist into his face. He keeled over, grabbing his mouth and jaw, as I fell to my knees, coughing.

"I should've killed you a long time ago," Istu told me.

I found the axe and picked it up.

"Exactly what I was thinking," I said, pulling back and then hurling the axe at him.

Here it was, my friends. The hero of the journey, with one last gasp, taking his weapon and destroying the final enemy with a heroic and grand gesture.

Except, the axe went flying into the woods behind Istu.

Istu picked up the knife and held it in his hands.

He laughed.

Then started toward me.

He was about to say something when a shot rang out, then another.

And then Istu's grin disappeared as his hand let go of the knife and he clutched his chest.

Blood flowed out of his chest, not in one place but in two.

I turned and looked back at the true hero of the story, holding the rifle in her hands, her wild hair tangled above her fiery eyes, staring ahead with a look that said one thing.

This is for my brother.

Max was in the dugout, already in the middle of the river.

"Kate, get in the boat!"

I turned to get the knife from Istu, and as I took it, gave him one last look. His eyes were wide in an expression of horror and surprise.

I took the knife and headed toward the boat. Kate was waist-deep in the water, almost to the dugout.

"Henry!" Kate called out.

I thought the other Indian had run away. But for some reason, he had decided to fire off one last arrow.

It found its way into my thigh.

I grimaced and stopped, falling on my knees again as I turned toward the jungle. I couldn't see him.

For a second I saw the blood spreading across my pants, dripping down my leg.

It hadn't hit the artery, thankfully. But it was wedged in deep enough.

In blinding, red-hot agony, I pulled it out.

Then I hobbled toward the dugout, still carrying the knife, blood running down my leg, sweat running down my face and neck.

I heard Kate's cries of surprise, made it to the dugout, and blacked out.

ON THE RIVER

We had stopped the bleeding with half of Max's shirtsleeve. I sat between Max and Kate in the dugout, alternating between sleep and drowsy consciousness, my bloody leg sticking out of the canoe. It was the afternoon, and my entire body ached. I felt as though I had lost a lot of blood. I would try and sit up, then felt lightheaded, needing to rest.

"Are you okay?" Kate asked from behind me.

"Sure, I'm fine."

We played this tune several times until Kate told me I was lying, and I told her that she was correct.

"Do you want to stop?"

I wiped the sweat off my forehead. "I'm just tired, that's all. I feel weak and dizzy."

"I'm looking for a good spot where we can camp for the night," Max said. "I'll give this fishing gear a try."

I looked at Max and at the crude tackle that he referred to, which we'd found lying in the bottom of the canoe. "You can't catch a fish with a regular fishing pole. What makes you think you can get something with that?"

"I might dive and grab for fish myself," Max said. "We need some food. Especially you."

"Think we're far enough to be safe?" I asked.

"I'm not going to feel safe until we're on a ship headed to New York," Kate said.

I wanted to get farther down the river, through the jungle and this imposing wilderness. We were headed north, but that meant nothing. As far as I was concerned, we were lost and in trouble.

Staring at my thigh wrapped in the wet bandage, I knew it was a lot of trouble.

I blinked my eyes, but they didn't open. Like the slowly drifting water and the cool breeze and the softly blowing leaves on the trees, my eyes gently closed.

Next thing I knew, I opened them and saw Kate's upside-down face looking at me.

"Henry—you're feverish. We need to stop."

"If you wanted to lie in her lap, why didn't you just ask?" Max said, trying to keep the mood light.

I sat up and felt queasy. The jungle around me wobbled as though I were riding on a swing.

"I'm going to be okay," I said. "I just . . ."

"Right there—that sandbank looks good. Let's camp over there."

"I don't know why I feel so groggy."

"You just got shot with an arrow," Max said. "Not to mention that you're probably dehydrated like the rest of us."

"He's pale and has a high fever," Kate said.

As we stepped off the boat, I fell to my knees. Kate was next to me, helping me up.

"Come on," she said, then grunted. "You're heavy, you know that?"

"And you're tough, you know that?"

"Yes. I've heard that before. I think from you."

I felt something shift in my pants pocket. I took out the dark rock.

"Hey—good news," I told them. "I still have my flint. At least we'll have fire."

We did have fire. Until the rains hit. And this was the worst downpour yet.

As the rain started, we went into the jungle to find some sort of shelter. A large tree provided some, and we all huddled together as the rain fell down and blew in sideways. We didn't have any blankets or extra clothes, and it was cool out.

I shivered. The last thing I needed was to be soaked and chilled throughout the night. My wound had gone numb, but my fever and ache were worse.

About ten minutes into the storm, the rain was so heavy it didn't feel like droplets but like endless streams pouring out of giant spigots in the sky. It seemed to last forever, but it finally tapered off and left us in eerie, dripping silence.

I heard Max cough out an angry laugh, then get up from where he sat. Kate was cushioned between the two of us.

"The dugout. I forgot to tie it up. Hope it hasn't already gone downstream."

He took off, and I continued to fight off the convulsions.

Kate snuggled up beside me and put both her arms around me. As the clouds moved away with the swiftness of the rains they had brought, I could see her faintly in the darkness. Maybe it was just my memory and imagination, but I could see the strength in her face and in those eyes.

"Are you okay?" she asked me.

"Never been better," I said as my teeth chattered from the cold.

"Don't get any ideas," she said.

"You're the one holding me. What ideas could I possibly get?"

"You're shivering so badly."

"I'm nervous. You should see what I'd do if we kissed."

"That's not funny."

Kate held on to me, her face gently touching mine. Her mouth was up against my ear.

"You're going to be okay," she said in a soft voice.

"I'm okay now."

"No, you're not," she said. "You're sick."

I moved away from her and could see the rain dripping off her cheek and her nose.

"This is a long way from New York, huh?"

She laughed, and I recalled her eyes, dark and penetrating. She was beautiful. She was beautiful the first time I met her, and she was even more so many miles deep in the forest. I didn't need light to picture her beauty.

"This is a long way from Rio," Kate said.

"Can I kiss you?" I asked.

"Henry . . ."

"Blame it on the wild fever. The rain. The near-death experience. Whatever. I don't want to die never having kissed you."

"You're not going to die."

"Kiss me," I said to her.

She looked down, her lips tightening.

And I moved in and kissed those lips gently, slowly.

A noise came out of the jungle.

"I leave you two alone for just a few minutes and look what happens," Max said. "Got any room down there under the tree?"

Kate pulled away, and I looked at her. She was speechless. I smiled.

I was a lucky man.

The rains didn't come back, but we were cold and soaked for a long time. I woke up at one point stretched out on the sand next to a blazing fire. Half of my body crispy, the other half clammy. I remember thinking this, then thinking I was definitely losing my mind.

"Kate?" I called out.

"I'm here," she said. "It's okay."

"Are you okay?"

"I'm fine. Go to sleep."

So I did.

But I would awake feeling worse, knowing my sickness wasn't going to get better any time soon.

I woke feeling stiff and cold. My fever was still there, but I didn't feel as dizzy. For a while I lay there next to the smoldering embers. I finally sat up and saw Kate standing at the edge of the water, the sun beaming down on her wild and wavy her.

"You okay?" I called out to her.

She turned around and walked toward the fire, and sat down next to me. "I'm fine. Max has gone fishing. How are *you*?"

"I had the wildest dream," I said. "It rained like a monsoon, then afterward you decided you wanted to kiss me."

"You have a wild imagination," she said, her eyes warm and inviting.

"Do you think Max will catch anything?"

She shook her head. "I doubt it."

I knew this was probably the best time to talk to her about her brother.

"I'm sorry about Louis," I said.

She looked back out at the river as though she had already been lost in thoughts of him when I'd called to her.

"It's what we thought we'd find, right? I knew that was a possibility. I just didn't realize . . . To make it that far, and then discover the truth like that . . ."

"I'm sorry," I said.

"I'm sorry too. He didn't deserve to die like that. Nobody deserves to die like that."

Her eyes were teary. I moved close beside her and took her hand. It was cold.

"Ruth told me something right before we got into the pool. She wanted me to know—she wanted *you* to know, in case something happened to her. I think maybe she went into that pool knowing she was going to die. I don't know. But I know what she said about Louis."

Kate looked at me, confused. "What?"

"She'd spent a lot of time with him. Ruth lost her husband when they decided to crucify him, hoping he would come back to life. Hoping he'd bring salvation, or something like that."

"And is that what they did with Louis?"

I sighed and nodded. "And what they tried to do with Max. They know the story well. They even cut their victim so he can bleed. That's part of the story, right? They did that to Max."

"And to Louis?"

"Yes. But Ruth was imprisoned with Louis for a while. She got to know him. And she talked to him about the Bible. About 'the Gospel,' she said. And I guess he believed all that stuff before he died."

Kate looked at me, her eyes wide and teary. "Are you—is that all she said? What else?"

"Just that. That's what she said. He understood 'the Gospel.' I guess he died understanding it. She desperately wanted you to know this."

"Why didn't you tell me this sooner?"

"Because—I didn't want to say it in front of Max. He's not the most—receptive person, I should say, when it comes to subjects like this."

"And you?"

"It doesn't matter what I think."

Kate wiped away her tears. "What *do* you think, Henry? Tell me."

"It doesn't matter. It's just—that's good about Louis, right?"

"Yes, it's good. But what do you think?"

"I think it doesn't matter, because he's dead. Whether or not he died believing in something is irrelevant. And I'm sorry. I'm so sorry, Kate. Those Indians were crazy. They believe in something too. Faith is a dangerous thing."

"Louis died with hope."

I didn't want to share what I thought. *He died deluded.*

"He died knowing where he was going," she said.

I nodded, not wanting to hurt Kate, not wanting to add to her pain.

But whether or not he knew where he was heading didn't matter. The moment he closed his eyes for the final time was it.

End of story.

Period.

"Henry, look at me," Kate said. "I care about you."

I laughed. "I know you do. But if you want to save me, get me out of this jungle."

"Maybe I will."

"Okay, then do it," I said.

She looked different. Lighter, almost.

The information about her brother certainly changed things for her.

And that was good. It sounded foolish to me, but if it made Kate happy, or at least more at peace with the news, that made me happy.

"Ruth said he was courageous to the last minute of his life," I said.

"I didn't need someone to tell me that," Kate said, looking up toward the heavens. "He was always brave. He was my baby brother."

As she looked up toward the sky, I wondered if she believed that Louis was looking down on her.

Maybe he was up in heaven and maybe he was looking down on us.

If you are, help us out a little, I thought as the waves of dizziness coursed through my body.

Kate continued holding my hand.

We had a long road ahead of us.

ON THE BOAT

February 8, 1929

I lost all sense of the day and the time and the place.

I remember at one point looking up and seeing the sky. The beautiful blue sky with its bursts of white peppered throughout.

I felt like I was moving, and I looked to one side and saw the tops of ancient trees passing.

All this way, and I'd been unable to soak in the sanctuary and solitude of this paradise.

A slight wind drifted across my cheek and forehead.

The sound of water lapped up, stirred, stroked made me drift off.

I felt peace.

Perhaps I've died and this is heaven, I thought.

But I looked up and saw a face, my dear and my protector, my guardian angel.

"You're going to be okay," she said.

And I believed her.

We were together in heaven.

I didn't want to go home.

I wanted to stay resting in her lap, heading downstream to never-never land.

"Henry?"

"Call me Henry."

"Henry, stay strong, okay?"

"Can we pet the jaguars?"

"We think there was poison in that arrow."

"Call me Henry."

"Henry, just stay with me. It's going to be okay. I'm praying for us, praying for you."

"Tell God I said hi."

"Henry, it's going to be okay."

"I'll have the duck."

"Henry?"

"Call me Henry."

"I love you. You crazy, chaotic soul. I love you. You can't go anywhere."

"I love you, and I love Max. I love the world."

"Keep fighting, Henry."

"Call me Henry."

The darkness wasn't really dark. And the silence wasn't really silent.

I saw the blinding desert and saw Max holding Kalila in his arms.

Never again, Henry, never again. God took her from me, and I'll get my revenge.

I could see Max's tears streaming down his dusty face.

"God didn't take her from you," I said.

Max yelled at me. *Yes, he did, and I swear I'll make him pay.*

"He's not there, Max. It's easier believing he's not there."

Yes, but that's still faith, Henry. You're still believing in something. Even if that something is nothing.

"I'm sorry," I said, oddly echoing another apology I'd given.

An apology I'd given even though it wasn't my fault.

You're not the one to say that. But I know who is. And I know where to find him.

And I looked up and saw stars moving in the sky.

I moved with them.

It was so hot.

Stifling.

I couldn't breathe.

I couldn't swallow.

My legs and arms felt numb.

"Stay strong, Henry."

I opened my eyes and saw cloudy skies.

I looked up and saw Kate. I tried to sit up, but she gently pushed me back.

"Don't—it's okay."

"Where are we?"

"Just rest. It's okay."

So I did.

". . . Father, be with us. Protect us. Please extend your grace over us, Lord, and bring us out of this darkness. Lord, we look up to you, we ask you, we beg of you to save us. Please, God, help us, bring us out of this darkness, Lord, please, we pray in your Son's name. . . ."

I jerked myself awake.

I sat up and looked around.

The grass I rested on was empty. The fire had apparently gone out some time ago. It was early morning with the sky an angry collage of oranges and reds as the sun tried to nudge awake the sleeping clouds.

I couldn't see Kate or Max.

I stood up and ran toward the water.

The boat was gone.

I called out their names. Over. And over. And over.

My forehead and my back were sweaty, and my mouth felt like I was chewing on mushrooms.

"Kate!" I screamed out, falling to the ground.

They'd left me. They had finally left me.

"Henry?"

I looked toward the campsite.

"What are you doing?"

"I just—I thought—"

"Come back to the camp and sit down."

"Max? The boat?"

"He found some fish. We're finally going to get some food."

I walked back on uneasy legs and then found myself collapsing. Kate needed to help me back to the fire.

She looked at me as I sat there, scratching my thick beard and itchy neck.

"What?" I asked her.

"Last night was rough," she said. "I didn't think you were going to make it."

I coughed, a deep cough that sounded bad. My body still ached, my mind was still dizzy.

"I'm not sure if I'm through this yet."

She grabbed my hand. "You're resilient, Henry. We're going to get out of here."

"You know that to be true?"

"I believe it."

I nodded.

"Then keep believing," I said. "And don't leave my side."

OUT OF THE DEVIL'S MOUTH

February 11, 1929

The morning sun felt good against my dirty, worn clothes and my weary, worn body.

I awoke without a fever.

The ground felt familiar in its discomfort. The fire next to us still fizzed and sparked. I sat up and felt woozy. It seemed like I had been sleeping for days.

The beach was wide and the river the widest I'd seen it. It was tranquil and soothing to listen to.

I couldn't remember what it looked like not to see the surrounding forest or not to feel the daily climate on my clothes and to my very core. The animal sounds, varied as they were, loud and soft in waves, formed a backdrop as easily ignored as the sound of the wind.

I tried to get my eyes to open more, to get my head out of the clouds.

I remembered eating fish last night. Somehow Max had managed to get some.

Neither of them was around. I enjoyed the peacefulness. I longed for a cup of coffee to warm me up and wake me up.

I longed to go home.

And then, down the beach, a figure approached. It was Kate, her hair wet, her pant legs rolled up, her shoes in her hands.

She smiled at the sight of me sitting up.

Suddenly the cup of coffee didn't seem so necessary.

Nothing else seemed necessary. Not if I could awaken and see a vision like that coming toward me.

All the comforts of the world couldn't equate to being with Kate.

Not in the least.

"How are you feeling?"

"Like I just awoke from a coma."

Kate laughed. "Well, there were times we didn't know."

"Was it bad?"

She nodded, her face giving her away.

"Thank you," I said.

"For what?"

"For taking care of me."

She shook her head. "You managed to find your way around those caves and rescue Max and me."

"Okay, so we're even."

"It's not about being even," she said.

"Yeah, I know. I wasn't going to leave you guys there."

"And I wasn't going to let anything happen to you. Not if I could help it."

"Where's Max?"

"He's getting the hang of this fishing thing. Remember the fish last night?"

"Vaguely," I said.

"He caught a few large ones. It was perhaps the best meal I've had in my life."

"Hunger will do that."

"They were exquisite," Kate said. "Perhaps the fish taste better out here."

"Maybe. Any idea where 'out here' actually is?"

"No, but we're hoping we'll come to a village soon."

"Hopefully no Indian tribes with strange beliefs and an aversion to white people."

"Yes, hopefully," Kate said. She sat down beside me. "Do you remember—do you recall our conversation last night?"

"No. Not really. I remember yesterday morning. Thinking you guys had left me."

"You woke up in the middle of night."

"Did I do anything inappropriate?"

Kate laughed. "No. But you were feverish. Delirious."

"What's new?" I asked.

"You don't remember any of it?"

"No. Well, except asking you to marry me."

"Stop, I'm being serious."

"No. But whatever I said—delirious or not—I probably meant it. I don't have anything to hide."

"I know you don't. But I do."

I looked over at her. "You don't have to hide anything from me. I know this—that we're two people suddenly thrust on a crazy journey. I don't know Kate Prescott in her normal setting, not really. But I know Kate. I know who you are. There's nothing you need to hide from me."

"Maybe not."

Max was approaching now, several fish in hand.

"You're alive." He pretended disappointment. "I was hoping Kate and I could have these all to ourselves."

"Good to know I'm in capable hands."

"These hands are feeding you, my son. I'm getting the hang of the fishing gear. Primitive, but it works."

"I'd say," Kate said. "Give me your knife, and I'll start cleaning them."

"Hungry?" Max asked me.

"I get hungry when I'm nervous."

Kate glanced at me and smiled, taking the fish.

Before we ate, Kate asked to pray.

"By all means," I said. "Your prayers seem to be helping things out. At least from my standpoint."

Kate held both of our hands.

"Our Heavenly Father, thank you for this beautiful day and for another day of life. Thank you for the blessing of another meal and of another chance to breathe in fresh air. We pray that you'll continue to watch over us. Continue to heal Henry. Please, God, bring us out of this darkness and help us find someone to take us back home. God, you give us everything, and we pray that you'll continue to protect us. Show your face through the things that we cannot do. We ask this in your Son's name. Amen."

"Amen," Max said.

"Amen," I repeated.

So tell me about the last day or so."

"It's been a month since we left the Indian village," Max joked, eating his fish with both his hands.

"Feels like it could be, as far as I'm concerned."

"We've been on the river. Thankfully there have been no rapids. Yet. The river keeps getting bigger and wider. I'm hoping to run into one of the tributaries that head to the Amazon. If we do, then we'll find someone."

"You think so?"

Max nodded. "We got out of that city. If we can do that, we can do anything."

"How sick was I?" I asked.

"You even got me praying, you know that?" Max said with a laugh. "When the Frenchman starts to pray, the end of the world is nigh."

I nodded at Max. "Thank you."

"I'm telling you, it's the fish," Max said.

Kate agreed. "It's got a power in it."

"I won't disagree," I said working on my breakfast in between the two people who had saved my life.

I think that maybe, just maybe, that was the best breakfast I'd ever had in my entire life.

I knew that the unexplained did occasionally happen. God or luck or fate or whatever, things just happened.

But becoming gravely ill from a poisonous arrow and then getting over it, that was a miracle. Back home it was one thing, but here in the wilderness, battling the elements and exhaustion, with nothing to eat and no doctor or medicine—how else could I describe that?

It was a miracle, pure and simple.

But it wasn't the last one that day.

INTO THE SKY

February 11, 1929

At first I thought I was hearing something.

A buzzing sound, coming from above.

Then Kate let out a gasp and turned around toward me. I was in the center of the dugout, Kate and Max doing most of the paddling since I was still weak. She grabbed my hand and looked up.

Max and I followed.

And there it was. Beautiful, soaring, gliding down toward the wide river.

A yellow seaplane.

The pilot waved at us and we signaled back, screaming, howling, greeting him with outstretched arms.

Surely he saw how destitute we looked.

We all started to paddle wildly. The river opened up onto another river.

"I think we've just reached the outskirts of the Amazon," Max said.

The seaplane rose up and then turned around, leveling off in the big river in front of us and coming down.

Kate started to cry. I moved up and put a hand on her shoulder, gripping tightly. I looked back at Max. He looked exhausted, for once out of witty words to say.

We were saved.

We guided our dugout next to the seaplane, where the pilot had climbed out and stood on the edge. He was an old ex-Air Force guy with, amazingly, more facial hair than I had. His side of our first conversation sounded something like this:

"You're from where?"

"What happened again?"

"What kind of city was that?"

"The Indians did what?"

"You've been out here for how many days?"

It soon grew too much for Kate, who yelled at him. "Just take us to the nearest city!"

"Yeah, sure, no problem," he said. Then, looking at me, he added, "You don't look too good, mister."

"Yeah, near-death doesn't do much for my complexion."

He looked at me, apparently ready to ask another question, then looked at Kate and changed his mind. "Manaus is just over those mountains. I can take you there."

We didn't say much as we climbed into the aged seaplane. It looked like a large tin boat with a giant wing and three-wing propeller attached to it. If I hadn't seen it flying just moments earlier, I would have doubted it could take off.

There was room for five inside, so Max sat next to the pilot and Kate and I took seats behind them.

The takeoff was bumpy, but I didn't worry about it. It would just be my luck to survive Chicago thugs and killer vines and a flying leap off a cliff, among other things, and then have our seaplane crash.

I looked out and could soon see the tops of the trees and the miles of surrounding jungle. In the distance I could see mountains. The same mountains we had just come out of. The view was glorious and moved me. I was tired and sick and hungry and depleted, so this was probably what brought tears to my eyes.

I looked over at Kate. Surely her fatigue was doing the same for her.

I smiled at her.

Then I grabbed her hand and held it as we flew higher.

MANAUS, BRAZIL

February 13, 1929

We stood in front of the famed Teatro Amazonas, the great and opulent opera house. It was reminiscent of the Italian Renaissance style, and conjured up images of Florence rather than a city in the middle of the rainforest, nine hundred miles inland from the Atlantic coast. Kate fit the picture in her glowing white skirt and jacket, with a matching hat. She looked like she was banishing any dirt from her life with this unmistakably clean outfit.

"Hello, Henry," she said, somewhat formally.

"I'm sorry, do I know you?"

She laughed. "How are you?"

"The sleep has been good. So has the food."

"That's good. You look—you look well."

"Amazing what a bath and a shave can do for a man."

There was a strange reserve in our conversation. We were no longer in a dugout, in grubby clothes, starved and sleep-deprived. We were no longer a team out there battling the wilderness. We were back to the people we used to be.

"I'm leaving on a plane today. My father chartered it. I tried to get Max to agree to come, but he wants to stick around for a while."

"Yes, he told me. I'm going to stay as well. Someone needs to keep him out of trouble."

"I understand," Kate said.

"How is your family, considering everything?"

She sighed. "It's been quite an ordeal, because of the press. I've even had people trying to interview me here. It's ridiculous. They need to allow a family to grieve."

"How are you?"

She nodded and smiled. "I'm well, thanks."

"Really?"

"Yes, really."

"I feel as though there should be something more. That we should have at least come back with an artifact or a treasure or something."

"We did," Kate said, peering at me from underneath her wide hat.

"What?"

"We discovered what happened to Louis. We came back with the truth."

"The truth?"

"Yes. And I can rest better at night knowing it."

"Why? Because in the last moments of his life, he decided to believe in God?"

"Still don't believe, do you?"

"It's irrelevant whether or not I believe. But I know that when you're about to die, you're willing to believe in a lot of things."

"Really? Like what?"

I thought of kissing Kate, of her holding me, of hearing her say she loved me in my dreams.

I wondered if those were the dreams and fantasies of a fever-riddled mind or if she really, truly had said those words.

Seeing her in front of the opera house, a building that she could easily have found herself sitting in, I knew that she and I were not meant to be together. She belonged to that world. I belonged in another.

"You can believe a lot of things when you're about to die. But reality is another thing, and if you're given a chance to make it out alive, you reconsider those foolish notions."

"I don't believe my brother's faith was foolish," Kate said in an irritated tone.

"I'm not talking about your brother's faith."

I'm talking about mine, I thought. Faith in something being there, something more, something between us.

For a second Kate looked at me and tried to make sense of what I was saying.

"I'm glad you found the truth," I told her, letting it go.

Letting her go.

"I wish you would discover it too."

"There are a lot of things I discovered along this journey. It's going to take a while to figure out what they really mean."

"Will you write about this?"

"Of course," I said, with a smile. "Lots to write about."

"And what will Henry Wolfe say about Kate Prescott?"

"You'll have to wait and read for yourself."

"Be kind."

I laughed. She didn't understand. But that was okay. She didn't need to.

"I'm sorry we weren't more successful, Kate."

"I am too. Thank you for rescuing me."

"I can say the same thing to you, you know."

She smiled. And, oh my, was she ever radiant and lovely. Kate— you're a vision, and if you don't know that, it's okay, because you are and you always will be. And you're not just a vision in white standing in front of an opera house, you're a vision in the rain all wet and muddy and tired. You're a vision.

Is that kind enough?

"So, Kate," I said. "Did you pray for me when I was in the boat? When I was sick?"

"Of course."

"Well, then, thanks for that also. And thank God for me when you get a chance."

"You can do that yourself, Henry."

"Please, call me Mr. Wolfe."

"When will you and Max be leaving?"

"Probably in a few days. There's a boat that'll take us to the Atlantic. We'll get to spend some time looking out at the sea. I won't mind. Not this time. I just hope it's safe for me to go back home."

"It's never safe where you are," Kate said.

"Maybe I need to stay around you. You have God on your side."

She laughed. "Yes. And he's given me the wisdom to stay clear of scoundrels like you."

"I like that. It makes me sound so—so rugged and handsome."

"No, it makes you sound like a criminal," she said, with laughter in her voice.

She glanced at the edifice behind us, the winding stairs that led up to the front doors. "In another life, it would have been nice to be standing here, getting ready to go inside," she said.

"Yes. Another story, perhaps. But I quite like the going-over-the-falls image myself."

She laughed. "I still can't believe that happened."

"Me neither. It's hard to take it all in. And that right there is the reason I'm a writer. To document it and try to make sense of it."

Kate smiled at me, then gave me a hug. "Good-bye, Henry."

"For now," I said, taking one last long look into those treasured eyes.

I kept telling myself it wasn't a big deal, that this was part of the journey, that Kate was always destined to go back to her life and so was I. We were both still wanted back home. But the people that wanted me wanted to kill me.

I knew I'd be seeing a lot of Max the next week, so I kept my distance in Manaus. For the next couple of days I wandered the large, exotic city alone, collecting my thoughts, collecting my heart.

I should've been with someone.

I should've been with her.

On the day our ship was to leave on the Negro River, heading down the Amazon to the Atlantic Ocean, Max brought an American newspaper to breakfast.

"Looks like you might be able to go back home after all," he said.

The story detailed the execution of seven men on the north side of Chicago, six reported to be members of Bugs Moran's gang. It mentioned Al Capone's possible involvement, but said he was reported to have been in Florida at the time.

"Can you believe it?" Max asked.

I shook my head. "There are too many killings in Chicago. Maybe I'll stay away for a while."

"So where are you going to write your next bestseller?"

I sipped my coffee, a luxury I was still not taking for granted. "How about Key West?"

He laughed. "Yeah, right. Want to get killed there?"

"Where are you headed?" I asked.

"I haven't thought that far ahead."

"Let me guess—you've met a lady down here."

"How'd you know?"

I shook my head. Some things never change.

But I thought of Kate and knew that some things do.

ON BOARD THE *PRINCESS*

February 19, 1929

Max walked up next to me wearing a sharp khaki suit.

"Settling in for the long journey?" I asked.

Max nodded, looking serious for some reason.

"I don't like that look on your face," I said.

"You shouldn't. Ever feel like you've had déjà vu?"

"Not recently."

"I just did. Someone's watching us."

"Didn't this happen last time we were on a ship?"

Max nodded. "Déjà vu."

"Who you do you think it is?" I scanned the deck around us. The wind from the ocean blew against my hair.

"I think they're working for the same person the first group were working for."

"You really think Richter sent guys to watch us again? The expedition is over."

"Not for Bernard Richter. It's never going to be over for him."

I nodded, thinking back to the final conversation I'd had with him in the African desert. "Seems like another universe, doesn't it?"

"Yes, it does," Max agreed.

"It'll be a little harder to relax now," I said.

"I'll relax just fine."

"Passing out from drinking is not what I'm talking about."

"I never pass out. I just take small naps."

For a while we looked out at the ocean, lost in thought. I finally broke the silence.

"What do you make of everything that happened? Does it make sense to you?"

Max laughed. "I haven't tried to think too much about it."

"It just—some of the things we saw. Some of the things that happened. It makes me wonder."

"Wonder about what?"

"About a lot of things."

"Faith? God? Magic?"

"All of those things."

"Maybe that's good," Max said.

"And you? What are your thoughts?"

"About what?"

I shrugged. "Faith. God. Magic. Do you believe that there was something else out there—some force helping us make it out? Some force helping those Indians?"

"Sure. I believe in those forces. And—well, all I can say is that God and I are friends again."

I stared out at the vast ocean and the endless sky. I had more questions than I'd had before starting out on this journey.

"I don't know."

"What don't you know?" Max asked.

"If there's a God. And if someone like Kate is so much different from those Indians back in the cave."

"Last I saw, she wasn't kidnapping people and tying them up on crosses."

"Yeah, but she believes in this whole—this thing. Look at that missionary woman we met. Ruth. Her husband died, and so did she. Is she a hero? Are they heroes now?"

"Depends on who you ask."

"I'm asking you," I said. "Last I saw you're the only person around here I'm talking with."

"You're a bit testy, you know?"

"All I know is that I'm absolutely confused. I thought I understood things after Egypt."

Max looked at me. "You decided to not believe in anything."

"That's right."

"And now?"

"Now I don't know. I have a hundred questions."

"Then maybe you need to embark on a few more adventures. Maybe you'll discover what you need to learn."

"And maybe I won't be so lucky next time, and I'll end up dying in the middle of nowhere."

"If that's your destiny, then so be it."

"What if destiny doesn't exist?"

Max finished his cigarette. "Such deep questions."

"It's hard for them to be anything else after that journey."

"There's just one thing I don't understand," Max said. "Something that truly shakes the foundations of my beliefs."

"What's that?"

"How could you let someone like Kate Prescott walk away?"

I looked at him. I wanted to say many things, but all I could do was laugh.

"I don't think I had a choice in that," I said.

"Are you going to chase after her?"

"What do you mean, chase after her?"

"I mean exactly that," Max said. "You could take a hundred more journeys and never find a woman like her."

"I know that."

"And yet here you are, stuck on a boat with an old Frenchman." He shook his head and muttered something in French.

"What'd you say?" I asked.

"It's just an expression. Something along the lines of 'no matter how much things change, some things always remain the same.' Look at us. Here we are again. No treasure in hand. Neither of us got the heroine. This is not the best way to end adventure tales, Henry."

"Tell me about it," I said. "Next time we have to come back with *something*."

Max laughed. "No, sir. No next time for me."

"What do you mean?"

"I mean, I've had my share of adventures. I'm getting too old. I'll let you continue your search for God and for meaning and for the next great find."

"You're going to let me die out in the middle of nowhere?"

"If you're crazy enough to go there, that's up to you. If I were you, I'd head to New York City."

"Oh, you would, would you? And what would you find there?"

"A feisty, irresistible woman, who for some reason is madly in love with you."

"Do you think so?" I asked him.

He shook his head. "Have I not taught you anything?" He walked away, saying something else in French.

I stood looking out at the ocean and the fading sun.

She was out there, somewhere, and she seemed to have some answers.

Maybe, just maybe, I'd go find her again.

AUTHOR'S NOTE

most authors, especially those who always show up on the best-seller lists, stick with one genre. Publishers like this, as do many readers. That's because you know what to expect once you're lounging by the beach and starting to read. *She writes such great love stories. His books make me scared of the dark.* You know and trust the author, so you know where they will take you when you go on another journey with them.

If you've followed any part of my writing career, you'll notice that I don't stick in one genre. In fact, I've done my best to try writing all sorts of stories. The primary reason I've done this is because I love a variety of genres—suspense, love, horror, and yes, adventure. But another reason I'd like to share is because of what publishers want or don't want.

Out of the Devil's Mouth was initially pitched as a dark, brooding story in the vein of *Heart of Darkness* by Joseph Conrad or the movie version, *Apocalypse Now*. I wanted to tell a story of an ill-fated trip down a river into the forbidden wilderness of the jungle. Supernatural events terrorize the crew. I saw a missionary upstream either being held hostage or perhaps having gone mad (a la Kurtz in Coppola's *Apocalypse Now*). At the time, this was going to be the follow-up to my supernatural suspense story entitled *Isolation*. My editor and I both agreed to the idea, and he suggested possibly having the story take place in the 1920s or 30s when traveling in the Amazon jungle was truly remote.

As it turned out, *Isolation* would be on hold for a while for reasons I won't get into here. But that changed the direction of *Out of the Devil's Mouth*. The publisher didn't want another dark tale from me (like *Isolation*), yet my editor didn't want a sweet love story like *The Promise Remains* (my first novel published). So I rethought the initial story and with the help of my editor, we came up with this tale very much in the vein of *Raiders of the Lost Ark*.

Because of my desire to write various stories, I didn't initially want to do a series. But I approached Henry Wolfe and this book as though it was book two in a series. If you're wondering where the first Henry Wolfe book is (the one that's been referred to multiple times in this book), well, you don't need to ask the author or the publisher. It exists in the dark, black hole of my mind. One day it might see the light of day, but we'll have to wait and see.

Because of the publishing industry being the way it is (and if you're wondering about my views on that, read *Sky Blue*), I'm not sure if there will be more Henry Wolfe tales. I have many more stories in

mind for him—different locales, different characters, different plots
—but we'll have to see. I grew to love Henry, as well as Max and
Kate. And even though this wasn't the *Heart of Darkness* tale that I
first thought it would turn out to be, I immensely enjoyed writing
this story. And I hope you enjoyed reading it.

As far as what's next, all I can say is stay tuned. If I spelled out
all the ideas and stories I have swirling around in my head, it would
probably give you a headache. I could give you five stories I'm dying
to write, but only time will tell if they get written down. Perhaps
some of those stories will, but not in the initial way I imagined them.
Writing, creating, and publishing are all fascinating and frustrating
at different times. But that's what makes the process so exciting.

So I thank you for taking another journey with me. I don't ever
want to take this for granted—the fact that I can spin tales and
hopefully move the reader in some way. That's what I'm always going
for. That and the chance to do something different. Keep reading,
and keep taking chances on different stories. You never know what
you might find along the journey.

Travis Thrasher
January, 2008

TRAVIS THRASHER is the author of eight previous novels. In third grade, while attending school in Munich, Germany, Travis decided he wanted to be a writer. He wrote his first novel in ninth grade when he lived in the Smoky Mountains of western North Carolina. He currently lives with his wife and daughter in a suburb of Chicago.

When his first novel, *The Promise Remains,* was released in 2000, *Publisher's Weekly* called it "one of the nicest surprises in CBA fiction." Never one to repeat the same old formula, Travis has written novels in several genres including suspense, adventure, and drama. He strives not to be put into an artistic box, both with his faith and with his stories.

Having worked in the publishing field for over 13 years, Travis is a full-time writer and speaker. For more information about Travis, visit www.travisthrasher.com.

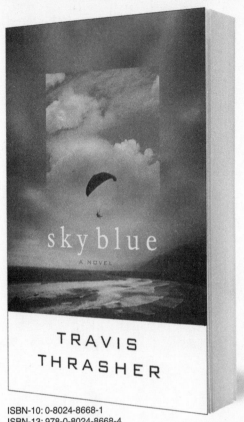

ISBN-10: 0-8024-8668-1
ISBN-13: 978-0-8024-8668-4

Open Your Eyes...

Colin Scott reads people for a living. They bare their souls on paper and he sells them to the highest bidder. His work as a top literary agent representing big name authors has turned his youthful ambitions into everything he has every wanted.

But Colin's passion for molding new writers into proven talent has somehow become aggravating and routine. On top of this mounting cynicism and professional monotony, Colin and his wife are desperately trying to have a baby.

Every decision he has ever made now has a question mark after it. And his usually clear-cut motivations are leading toward a nervous breakdown.

And then, on a much-needed escape to Cancun, tragedy strikes. Colin's life is irrevocably changed.

by Travis Thrasher

Find it now at your favorite local or online bookstore.

www.MoodyPublishers.com

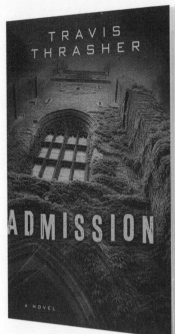

ISBN-10: 0-8024-8672-X
ISBN-13: 978-0-8024-8671-4

ISBN-10: 0-8024-8671-1
ISBN-13: 978-0-8024-8672-1

Some Secrets Find You . . .

As Jake Rivers got on with his life after college, there were some things that could not just be left alone—like a certain spring break trip gone really bad. And now, 11 years later, he is given another chance to search for the truth in his past.

Alone in NYC . . .

Alone in New York on a business trip, Michael risks his perfect life for a seductive smile from a stranger. A simple conversation and a short phone call plunge Michael into a night out of his control. He starts by flirting with temptation and ends up fighting for his life.

by Travis Thrasher
Find it now at your favorite local or online bookstore.

www.MoodyPublishers.com

ISBN-10: 0-8024-1748-5
ISBN-13: 978-0-8024-1748-0

ISBN-10: 0-8024-1707-8
ISBN-13: 978-0-8024-1707-7

Convicts Running to a Small Town

Five escaped convicts run from the law and into the lives of some mysterious people. A woman running from another life. A father burdened with the sins of his past. A broken deputy who might be a hero. And a dangerous ringleader seeking control. With unanswered questions on the rise, a twist of fate leads to the place where all their paths will cross just one more time.

Why Me?

Tom is willing to sell his soul—or at least his employer's most closely guarded secret—to the highest bidder. But after surviving a deadly plane crash, he gets a second chance to redeem his past mistakes. With this new opportunity, will Tom choose to change?

by Travis Thrasher
Find it now at your favorite local or online bookstore.